RIDE WITH HATE

Buffalo hunter Miles Flint had good reason to hate Jonas Carlisle. A herd of stampeding Carlisle cattle had killed Flint's best friends and destroyed a fortune in buffalo skins. Yet Flint joined Carlisle's crew in their suicidal drive across the forbidden Indian territory to Montana. Did Miles want revenge? Did he want Carlisle's beautiful wife, Lorena? Or did he want both?

Beck Sterrett and Bat Batteau, Carlisle's lieutenants, both hated Miles Flint for reasons of their own. And both were determined to destroy him . . . for reasons of their own.

More SIGNET Westerns You Will Want to Read

THE LONE RIFLE

by Gordon D. Shirreffs

A SIGNET BOOK from

NEW AMERICAN LIBRARY

TIMES MIRROR

Copyright © 1965 by Gordon D. Shirreffs

FOURTH PRINTING

SIGNET TRADEMARK REG. U.S. PAT. OFF. AND FOREIGN COUNTRIES
REGISTERED TRADEMARK—MARCA REGISTRADA
HECHO EN CHICAGO, U.S.A.

SIGNET, SIGNET CLASSICS, SIGNETTE, MENTOR AND PLUME BOOKS
are published by The New American Library, Inc.,
1301 Avenue of the Americas, New York, New York 10019

FIRST PRINTING, MAY, 1965

PRINTED IN THE UNITED STATES OF AMERICA

CHAPTER ONE

The dry prairie wind had shifted as the sun moved westward across the Kansas plains. The clear morning sky had become dotted with slowly drifting clouds that threw fleeting shadows on the rolling, grassy terrain. To the north a shimmering heat haze had begun to form over the valley of the Smoky Hill River. A dun-colored mass drifted northwesterly across a wide, shallow valley south of the valley of the Smoky Hill, raising a thin cloud of bitter yellowish dust that settled on the cured buffalo grass like a great shaggy blanket.

The lone horseman reined his bay to a halt and then slid from the saddle. He carefully lifted the heavy, long-barreled Sharps rifle from its saddle slings and fitted the ten-power Vollmer rifle-telescope to the mounts atop the Sharps barrel. He padded softly up the sandy slope and lay bellyflat behind a clump of soapweed, removing his dusty hat before he raised his head above the lip of the low ridge. A fleeting grin passed across his brown face. *"Cibolo!"* he said. The wind had shifted just as he had predicted it would with the coming of the greater heat of the July day. It was now blowing from the vast herd of grazing buffalo directly toward him.

Miles Flint slid down out of sight and levered open the breechblock of the heavy rifle, placing a big paper-patched cartridge into the chamber of the converted Sharps, closing the breechblock, and setting the hammer at half cock. He carefully checked the rifle telescope, cleaning the good German lens with a camel's-hair brush. He bellied up the slope again and placed the *bois d'arc* buffalo sticks just between two clumps of soapweed, separating them to place the rifle barrel in the upper crotch of the sticks. He rested the butt of the rifle on the ground and lighted a cigar. He drew in a few deep breaths of the smoke and then tossed the cigar down the slope to a bare patch of the sandy soil, watching the thin smoke waver upward and then drift with the wind. He nodded, then placed

5

a score of fat-bellied brass .45-120-550 cartridges on a flat rock close to hand. Miles unfastened his big, cloth-covered canteen and placed it beside the rock.

The wind was a little variable but blowing almost directly from the herd toward Miles. He would need no windage. He studied the herd through the powerful rifle 'scope. An old cow stood fifty yards closer to him than the rest of the herd, a good two hundred and fifty yards from Miles's "stand." He wanted to work closer, but there was no cover between him and the herd. Miles knelt on the slope, gripped the buffalo sticks with his left hand just below the crotch of the sticks, and sighted on the unsuspecting cow. He used the upper crosshairs, then slowly took up the trigger slack. He took in a deep breath, held it, then let out half of it. He settled the upper crosshairs for a lung shot and squeezed off. The rifle roared, spitting flame and smoke; driving powerfully back into the hollow of his shoulder. He peered through the smoke that blew back into his lean face. The cow had been hit. She moved ahead a few feet, then suddenly went down on her foreknees. The bulls nearest her raised their heads at the smell of the blood and moved closer, sniffing at her. One of the younger bulls hooked at her with his horns. Miles nodded. They were more interested in her than they were in the cause of her strange behavior.

Miles reloaded. From now on it would be heart or neck shots to cause quick death. He fired swiftly, almost casually, but each of his actions was that of the skilled professional. The smoking, empty brass hulls tinkled against the flat rock. A fresh round was slid into the chamber. A moment's hesitation and the Sharps roared. Each heavy slug struck its mark. The herd was getting nervous, raising their shaggy heads and sniffing the wind, but they held their ground until the sixth buffalo went down; then they began to mill a little. The bulls moved out to the flanks of the herd, the cows nuzzled the calves inside the protective ring.

Miles slid down the slope and poured water down the smoking barrel to clean the fouling. It looked like a damned good stand. He needed four more hides for that day's work. An excellent stand that morning had enabled him to get twenty-five hides from a smaller herd. His skilled Canuck skinners were still hard at work on them on a fork of the Smoky Hill where he had set up his camp, beyond a westward ridge and downwind of the bigger herd. Thirty-five a day was Miles Flint's quota. He had set it for himself in his four years of buffalo hunting. It was a good day's work for both Miles and his skinners—no more, no less.

He eased back up the slope and settled his rifle in the sticks.

6

As he did so he noted a thin wraith of dust beyond the eastward ridge of the shallow valley. He narrowed his gray eyes. He had thoroughly scouted that area the evening before and had seen no buffalo for miles. As far as he knew, no herd had moved into the area during the day, and it wasn't likely they had done so. He was at least twenty miles from the nearest camp of buffalo hunters. It wouldn't be Indians—they wouldn't advertise their approach like that. They were seen only when they wanted to be seen.

Miles fired again and dropped a massive bull. The herd was restless but holding its ground. Miles shifted his tobacco chew and spat to one side, eyeing that dust cloud. It was getting closer. If it was a buffalo herd—and he was almost positive that it couldn't be—they were moving far too fast for the normal movement of a herd from one grazing area to another. He rubbed his lean jaw and studied the dust. It was moving directly toward the herd he was working on. If the oncoming herd panicked the herd in the valley, they'd likely drive right down toward Miles's skinning camp on Smoky Hill Fork.

He downed a cow and a young bull. The herd began to drift to the north, rather than to the west, heading upwind as usual for the ridge that separated the valley from the valley of the Smoky Hill. Miles spat out his chew and stood up. It wasn't like buffalo to move toward higher ground, even upwind, unless they were frightened.

The dust swirled up thicker and thicker. Miles dropped to his knees and placed an ear close to the ground. His face tightened, and an uneasy feeling stirred his guts. A steady tremor came to him through the great sounding board of the earth. Something was moving toward the great buffalo herd; something moving on thousand of hooves and moving fast—too-damned fast! It was likely another herd, maybe stampeded by some damned fool playing at being a buffalo runner, a menace to every other hunter in the area.

Miles picked up his cartridges, slung his canteen, snapped together the buffalo sticks, and grabbed his rifle. It was time to move and stand not upon the order of his going. After casing the 'scope, he put the rifle in the slings. He swung up on the bay and turned eastward, a puzzled look on his lean face. He touched the bay with his heels and rode along the ridge crest, keeping out of sight of the herd as much as possible. Maybe they wouldn't be panicked and stampeded by the oncoming herd, and he could make a stand the next morning within close proximity to his skinning camp. The dust was swirling up thicker and thicker. If the running herd stampeded the valley herd and the combined herds drove west toward the fork of the Smoky Hill, there would be hell to pay and no pitch hot.

7

The bay tossed its head and whinnied sharply. Miles patted his neck. "You don't like it either, hey, boy?" he said quietly.

The dust was driving down into the valley now, swirling over the nervous herd. Slowly they turned away from the north ridge and swung uneasily at a fast walk toward the west, leaving the humped carcasses of their dead. The bulls swung out to cover the flanks of the herd, the cows and calves held within their protection. Dust rose from their thudding hooves to mingle with the sweeping dust of the oncoming herd, thickening on the freshening wind.

Miles quirted the bay down the side of the low ridge into the valley and then let the bay run free. It was faster, although infinitely more dangerous, to cut across the face of the oncoming herd. The herd was beginning to move faster, humping awkwardly up and down, clumped close together and shaking the ground with the impact of thousands of hooves. Miles freed his converted Remington six-shooter from its sheath. Five rounds of .44 soft-nose slugs could drop as many buffalo at extremely close range, but Miles prayed to God it wouldn't come to that.

The bay's hooves drummed on the harder ground of the valley floor, drowned out by the ominous thundering of the buffalo herd. The buffalo were running free now with their deceptive, awkward style, covering the ground at a rapid pace. The bay drew from the deep well of his stamina and kept well ahead of the herd. They reached the low rise at the west end of the valley. Miles looked back over his shoulder. Something had topped the eastern ridge. A great mass of movement, shrouded in swirling yellowish dust, pouring down into the valley on the heels of the last of the buffalo herd, blotting out the prairie grass until the whole valley was filled from one side to the other. The slanting rays of the sun shone on sweat-glistening hides of myriad colors and on the tremendous spreading horns of the beasts.

Miles stared in disbelief. "Longhorns!" he yelled. He plied the braided quirt with all his strength.

He began to yell as soon as he saw the distant camp, placed just beyond the dotted carcasses of the buffalo he had killed from his first stand that day. Most of them had been flayed of their heavy pelts, the naked bloody flesh of the carcasses shining greasily under the sun's rays. Thick clouds of buzzing flies swarmed around. The sun also glinted from the clear, shallow waters of the fork just beyond the pitched tents and Red River carts and the remuda of mules and horses. A thin wraith of smoke rose from the cookfire. Some of the Canucks were pegging out the green hides on the level ground north of the camp for curing under the hot sun.

8

Miles thrust the heavy Remington upward and fired three times, the big pistol bucking back hard into the fork of his hand. He saw the faces of the skinners turn toward him. Big Tom, the Negro *cocinero,* looked up from his cookfire. "Stampede!" screamed Miles at the top of his voice. He knew he couldn't be heard; the buffalo had already topped the rise behind him, ramrodded on by the longhorns behind them, a moving mass of living flesh, of death on the hoof for any living thing that stood in its way.

There was no time to save any equipment. Everything had to be sacrificed to get those four men free from the shaggy, dusty death that was roaring toward them at a speed almost approaching that of a horse. Everything must go. Hides, carts, tents, supplies, gear, and weapons. *Everything!* One of the skinners fought to free the mules from a cart harness, and another skinner ran out toward the picketed mules and horses.

"No! No!" screamed Miles.

A horn of the herd had swung in toward the fork, eating up yardage between themselves and the picketed animals. One after the other the mules and horses jerked free, the picket pins flying through the dusty air. In a moment one skinner was gone beneath the pounding, sharp-edged hoofs.

The man at the cart mounted a mule, but the frightened beast, smelling the herd, buckjumped and then sunfished, pitching off his unwanted rider. The skinner sprinted futilely toward the creek. Big Tom came out of a tent, hugging something to his chest. He ran for the lone tree that stood at the edge of the fork and began to clamber up it, impeded by his heavy burden. The buffalo herd swirled around a knoll just beyond Miles, that created a vacuum in the mass of frightened animals, and then they thundered over the campsite, raising a pall of dust that blotted everything from sight except the sunshot reflection from the horns of the beasts.

There was nothing else Miles could do but try to save his own life. The bay could outrun them just so long. Miles reined in the bay, flipped open the loading gate of the hot Remington, and rammed in four rounds just in time to slide from the saddle and face the onrushing herd. He raised the pistol like a duelist and fired at the nearest bull, about fifty feet away. The impetus of the bull and the weight of the herd behind him tumbled fifteen hundred pounds of dead buffalo almost at Miles's feet. He fired again, dropping a big cow behind the bull. The bay tugged at the reins wrapped around Miles's left arm and spoiled his third shot, but the fourth shot dropped a young bull that was veering in toward Miles. The shaggy shoulder butted the bay aside, and the tip of a horn lightly raked Miles's sweating face. He emptied the Remington just

9

in time for the thundering herd to pass around the tumbled buffalo, leaving a narrow V of open space where Miles held on to the rearing, plunging bay.

Miles tied his scarf across the eyes of the bay, feeling the strong body shiver in panic. The herd smashed past. The heat and dust of it seemed to fill the whole world. Miles buried his face in the bay's mane and prayed as he had not prayed since he was a Union soldier at Gettysburg the day the Texans had nearly swept clear over Little Round Top.

The dust was a living thing, coating Miles's face, filtering into his nose and eyes, coating his tongue, and burning his sweating flesh. The heat sickened him, and the ground trembled spasmodically beneath his feet, heaving and rocking, or so it seemed, as the minutes ticked past, mounting into a quarter, a half, and then into a full hour. It seemed to Miles that the stampede would never end. Once he risked a glance at the pounding masses streaming past the dusty blockade of flesh he had flung down before him and he saw that these were longhorns passing now, their great horns clashing and clacking together. The smell of them was different, too, and the heat of the massed bodies almost blistered his face.

Then he sensed, rather than noticed, a slackening in the onrushing masses. He raised his head, peering red-eyed through the swirling dust. Stragglers pounded past, and once he thought he heard a man yell; he hoped to God it was one of his men. The dust hung thick as a pall over the fork and the ground still trembled, but the stampede had passed Miles. Not a scrap of vegetation showed on the trampled ground. Over it all hung the stench of dust, heavy droppings of the frightened buffaloes and cattle, and the acrid smell of the beasts.

A sustained bellowing came to him from the ridge, and more longhorns pounded into the valley, their great shining horns catching the light of the sun through the dust. Somewhere within the dust pall arose a familiar sound. The piercing rebel yell came again and a horseman pounded past on the flank of the herd, muffled to the eyes in his bandana, Mex hat pulled low, driving his racing buckskin against the leaders of the herd, forcing them to turn ever northward toward the ridge beyond which lay the Smoky Hill. Other riders smashed through the dust, whooping and yelling, working the tons of moving flesh toward the ridge with professional skill. A handgun cracked again and again.

Miles slowly pulled his sweat-soaked scarf from his burning face. He wiped the dusty layers from his face and neck and then drank deeply of the tepid water in his canteen. He filled his hat and let the shivering bay drink from it. The wet hat felt gratefully cool against Miles's burning head. He slowly took a cigar and bit off the end in a savage snap of his jaws, lighting the weed with a thumbnail-snapped lucifer. His glacial gray eyes remained on that damnable herd that had driven the buffalo into a stampede. "Gawddamn them and their damned cows!" he spat out.

Miles reloaded the Remington and sheathed it. It was characteristic of him that he checked the heavy Sharps before he led the bay toward the fork. Gone were the clear, purling waters. Gone were the tules and the lone tree. Gone were the camp, hides, Red River carts, horses, and mules. *Gone were the four men. . . .*

It was almost impossible to tell where the prairie left off and the fork began, for both banks were a trampled mass of churned mud and water. It was almost impossible to tell where the camp had been, for the lone tree that had marked it had vanished. The ground still trembled, but the buffalo herd was now moving over a distant rise, leaving a shroud of bitter dust hanging in the air, shot through with sun rays, glistening golden against the dust. To the north, closer to the Smoky Hill, moved the mass of longhorns, now at a more sober pace, bellowing thirstily as they caught the scent of the water, clashing their great horns, some of which spread as much as seven feet across on the full-grown *ladinos*. Several horsemen were loping after the buffalo herd to round up the longhorns that had stampeded the buffalo and then joined in their maddened rush over the defenseless camp.

Miles shifted his cigar and looked up to see the white tilts of wagons rising above the eastern ridge, swaying and pitching as the mule teams pulled them down into the valley, while the whiplashes of the muleskinners popped like skirmishing fire. It was a big spread, judging by the number of wagons and the many horsemen that rode with the herd.

Miles watered the bay and walked back toward the spot where he thought the camp had been. Thousands of sharp-edged hooves, weighed down by tons of buffalo meat and beef, had cut and recut the ground until it was one indistinguishable mass, pocked like the surface of the moon, only a thousand times over in miniature. It was as though the herd had meant to smash the banks of the fork and everything on them back into the basic elements of Mother Earth.

Miles shoved back his hat. "Jesus God," he said softly and not irreverently. "They never had a chance." A bitter loneliness winged invisibly out of the dusty air to settle like a harpy on Miles's broad shoulders. He had worked with those four men for over four years, paying all the expenses and sharing fifty-fifty with them, when the average skinner got two bits a hide. He had faced other stampedes with them, prairie

11

flash floods, a blue norther or two, prairie fires, the "red buffalo" of the Plains, marauding bands of Comanches, Kiowas, Cheyennes, and thieving Pawnees. A rather ill-assorted but harmonious group, with three laughing Canucks and one big Missouri nigger who had been as close to being a real friend as Miles Flint, Illinois born and bred, had ever had. "Jesus God," he said softly again. The shock had not yet worn off to give way to the bitter hate that would surely come.

He knelt in the mire and picked up a scrap of buckskin that had a few blue, pink, and white seed beads clinging to it—likely a sleeve garter worn by one of the Canucks. He paced slowly through the mud. Here he found a splintered bit of the lone tree where Big Tom had pitifully sought shelter. Here he found a shattered wedge of the grindstone used to sharpen the skinning knives. There was something else in the mud, startlingly white against the darkness . . . the bones of a man's arm and part of the hand still partly clothed in bloody scraps of dark-skinned flesh. The pitiful relic, all that was recognizable of Big Tom, lay across a battered rectangle of brass-mounted wood. Miles pried the heavy box out of the mud. The lid was cracked clean through, but the contents were safe enough, likely shielded by Big Tom's body as he fell before the pounding hooves. He opened the lid and looked down upon his valued set of reloading tools; bullet mold, tool for decapping and recapping the spent brass shells, a swage for bullet resizing, and a bullet seater, plus other odds and ends for keeping his Sharps in prime condition as well as for fashioning the reloads for it. Big Tom had carried the box from the tent, thinking of it first, before he had thought of himself, for he had known how much Miles valued it.

Miles closed the lid and looked down at the bones. "Odd," he said quietly. "His bones are the same color as a white man's."

The stampeded herd was a low rumble of thunder to the west. The longhorns had slowed to a fast walk toward the waters of the Smoky Hill, the wagons trailing along behind them out of the swirling dust. Three horsemen were riding swiftly toward the lone man who stood in the mud and blood beside the fork.

"Yuh all right, mistah?" yelled one of the riders.

Miles did not answer. His big brown hand slid down to the worn walnut grip of his Remington. It had killed men before and it would kill men again. Texans most likely. He spat at the thought of Texans.

Two of the riders spurred forward, scattering gobs of mud from beneath their horses' hoofs. The thick beard of one of them moved in the wind of his passage. The third rider had slowed his mount to a walk, keeping his eyes on Miles.

It was then Miles noted that it wasn't a slim man at all, but a woman, riding sidesaddle, wearing a Confederate-gray full-skirted riding habit.

"Are you all right, sir?" asked the bearded man in a deep, almost melodious voice, certainly not the tone of a Texan. Sounded like an educated man, a rarity amongst Texans, or at least so Miles thought.

Miles looked coldly at the bearded man. "You've wiped out my camp," he said in a flat voice.

"I assure you it was not intentional, sir. My name is Jonas Carlisle, trail driver."

Miles studied the man. He had said "trail driver" as though it were an honor, an accolade bestowed only on the richly deserving. "Intentional?" said Miles softly. "You stampeded thousands of buffalo over my camp because of your cursed longhorns. No word of warning. Where was your scout? Your trail boss? Your points? Surely you don't drive thousands of longhorns through open country like this without an advance party of some kind. One man could have warned you of those buffalo and the fact that my camp was here on the fork."

The other man, much younger, leaned forward in his saddle and looked at Miles with cold blue eyes. His tone was Texas, with all its faults and virtues, when he spoke. "He *said* it wasn't intentional, mistah. Mistah Carlisle means what he says."

Miles knew he was dealing with a breed of man entirely different from Jonas Carlisle. He had met such men as this young Texan in other places and at other times, mostly in violence, peering through the swirling gunsmoke with the deadly whistling of the minie balls playing a threnody to the deeper cracking of the rifles.

"Yuh hear what I say, mistah?" said the Texan as softly as he could speak, but there was honed steel beneath the softness of it, like the whetted edge of a bowie knife.

Carlisle held up a hand. "Enough, Cotton," he said. "This gentleman has a right to be angry. I assure you, sir, we had no knowledge of buffalo hunters being out here in the Smoky Hill country."

Miles relighted his cigar, watching Cotton through the flare of the match and the smoke. "The name is Miles Flint," he said. "Buffalo hunters don't usually advertise where they are. Buffalo can panic easily enough as it is. A blowing leaf, a howling coyote, a careless shot can do it." Cotton's hard blue eyes held Miles's cold gray eyes just long enough for the quick measuring, quite often the only measuring a man could have of another before the more deadly measuring began over the cold, metal eye of a gun muzzle.

"I'll gladly pay for all damages," said Carlisle.

Miles nodded. "I knew you'd say that. Does your damned payment allow for the lives of four good men?"

The Texan shifted in his saddle, looking down at the last earthly relic of Big Tom. "Well, anyways," he said out of the side of his mouth, "one of them was a niggah, wasn't he? Lookit the meat on them bones."

Miles looked at the Texan. "Maybe he was a better man than you are, Texan," he said with studied insult.

The Texan went whitefaced as the deadly verbal glove struck at him. His right hand dropped to his pistol butt.

"Enough of this!" snapped Jonas Carlisle. His tone had changed, too. He was no gunslinger, no Texas fighting cock, no killing machine like the two men who faced each other in front of him, but there was steel in his tone; the steel of a man used to responsibility, used to giving orders and having them obeyed. "Cotton, you keep out of this! Mister Flint has reason to be angry. *You* do *not!*"

Cotton opened and closed his mouth, never taking his eyes from Miles. Those glacial eyes seemed to go over Miles inch by inch, taking stock, enough to imprint Miles Flint forever in his memory. Miles knew right then and there that Cotton would never forget what Miles had said . . . ever.

"Go back to the herd," said Carlisle to the Texan. "Get some of the boys. Go after those beeves that followed the buffalo herd. I want them back at the Smoky Hill by dusk."

Cotton nodded, touching the brim of his hat. He spurred his dun toward the fork, his long, white-blond hair flowing as he rode, his back ramrod-straight.

"Is he the trail boss?" asked Miles. "Or do you handle that chore yourself, Mister Carlisle?"

"He is not the trail boss, Mister Flint. Nor do I handle that chore. Beck Sterret is trail boss. Another Texan. One of the best, if not the *best* in the business."

"The best trail boss or the best Texan?" said Miles, almost idly.

"Both," said the woman as she reined in her mare beside Jonas Carlisle.

Miles took off his hat and removed the cigar from his mouth to look into the loveliest eyes he had seen in years—soft, lustrous brown, a velvety coloring that seemed to hold something deeply beneath it. Deep, oh so very deep . . .

"My wife, Lorena," said Carlisle with ill-concealed pride. "This gentleman is Mister Flint, Lorena."

She was at least fifteen years younger than her husband, slim as a girl, and even the riding habit could not conceal her womanly features. Nature had been more than kind to

14

Lorena Carlisle. Miles's appreciation of Jonas Carlisle as a man of taste moved up a few notches. "Lorena," said Miles quietly. "I've heard that name before."

She smiled quickly. "Around the campfiahs of the Army of no'the'n Virginia, perhaps, Mistah Flint?" she said softly, *proudly*. Texas pride, to be admired or hated, depending on one's viewpoint.

Miles nodded. "A lovely, haunting song, 'Lorena'," he said.

"You are a Confederate veteran then?" she asked expectantly. "Perhaps a Kentuckian or Missourian?"

Miles shook his head. "We heard them singing that song many times around their campfires at night," he said. His eyes held hers and could not look away.

A flitting shade of coolness crossed the oval loveliness of her face, and her eyes hardened a little, like dark amber, but they still held him.

Carlisle looked about on the trampled, muddy ground. "I can repay you for your material losses," he said with genuine feeling. "But I can never repay you for the fine men you have lost."

Miles looked up at him. "It is not your debt to repay."

Carlisle narrowed his eyes. "I do not understand, Mister Flint."

Miles looked toward the drifting dust of the distant cattle herd, now at the Smoky Hill, slaking their prodigious thirst after the long trail miles. The man responsible for the deaths of Miles's employees and friends was there with the herd, holding to his responsibility for the herd, not thinking of the men who had died because he had not kept a scout or point out ahead of his herd. That, too, was his responsibility.

Miles nodded. "You're a long way from railhead," he said. "Where are you driving them?"

The answer struck Miles like the blow of a fist. "Montana," said Carlisle quietly.

"That's loco!" said Miles.

"Nelson Story did it."

"Over six years ago," said Miles.

"With a handful of Texans," said Lorena proudly.

Miles turned and looked up into that proud, lovely face. "And split-breech Remingtons the Sioux had never run into before, plus at least *one* Yankee."

Carlisle looked at Miles with a trace of amusement on his bearded face. "I've never heard of any Yankee being with that drive except Story himself," he said.

Miles placed a hand on his heavy Sharps. "He had a Yankee meat hunter with him," he said.

"You?" asked the trail driver.

15

Miles nodded. "All the way north from Fort Laramie," he said.

Carlisle slapped a heavy hand on his thigh. "By God!" he said. He looked quickly at Lorena. "Sorry," he added. "What will you do now, Mister Flint?"

"*Quien sabe?* My hides are gone. My skinners and cocinero are gone. I'm wiped out except for my horse and rifle. I'll likely head back to Dodge for supplies, carts, wagons, skinners, and suchlike."

Carlisle leaned forward in his saddle. "I'll repay you for all your losses, as I said before. I cannot repay you for the men. Would you consider hunting for me on this drive?"

Miles shook his head. "You'll never get through," he said. "Red Cloud stands in the way. The Bozeman Trail is closed. No white man living can get past Red Cloud, leastways no man driving a herd of longhorns and trailing a bunch of wagons and a *woman*."

She seemed to start a little, as though he had struck a soft spot. He had gotten home to her at least. Damn her and her beauty and her overweening Texas conceit!

"I mean to get through," said Carlisle in a distant voice. "There is a great future in Montana. I have land there, a great deal of land in the best cattle country in the world. Story broke the way, and now the Sioux have closed it. Well, they cannot stand in the way of our progress. They cannot stand in *my* way, Mister Flint! They have closed the way, but someone must reopen it. *I* am that man! It is my destiny!"

Miles picked up the reins of his bay. "Alexander the Great had a destiny. So did Julius Caesar and Napoleon Bonaparte. Not too long ago Jeff Davis and Bobby Lee had a destiny. Something stood in their way. Do not trifle with destiny, Mister Carlisle. It has a mean habit of turning on a man."

Carlisle's mouth worked a little through his thick chestnut beard. The faraway look faded from his deep eyes. "Can I offer you the hospitality of my camp on the Smoky Hill?"

Miles nodded shortly. "You can."

"Ride with us, then."

Miles shook his head. "Ride on," he said over his shoulder. "I'll be along later."

Carlisle and his lovely young wife rode on, looking back from a low knoll toward the destroyed camp and the man who still stood there. Miles Flint stood with hat in hand and bowed head.

"He is praying for his dead, Jonas," she said.

Jonas Carlisle's eyes were half closed. "He has prayed for his dead before," he said, "in many places—on the battlefields of the war and out here on the Great Plains. He will accept

16

their loss as he has accepted the loss of others." Carlisle touched his horse with his spurs. "I have a destiny to the north," he added, almost as though talking to himself again. "And somehow I know that the destiny of that man, and mine, are inextricably bound together."

They rode on in the late-afternoon sunshine toward the wraith of dust above the distant Smoky Hill. Once Lorena looked back, but Miles was gone, riding to the west. She did not answer her husband, but she knew. *She knew* . . .

CHAPTER TWO

Miles Flint rode in from the velvety darkness to the west toward the glow of the campfires.

The mingled odors of bacon, bannock and beans, and strong coffee drifted along the quiet river, mingled with the pungent smell of the fires of buffalo chips, the *bois de vache,* or "wood of the cow." There was little wood along that stretch of the Smoky Hill. As Miles reached the faintly lighted rim of the firelight wash, sun-bronzed men, their hair hanging almost to their shoulders, raised their faces from the steaming mugs of coffee to look thoughtfully at the big Yankee they had heard about after the herd had been bedded for the night. They knew of his loss, but they had also listened to the terse words of Jess Morser, nicknamed "Cotton" because of his ash-white hair. The big Yankee's insult would not be forgotten. The man would have to be measured, and if he was found wanting . . .

Firelight reflected from the faded white tilts of the three fine Studebaker wagons that had been drawn apart from the chuckwagon and the supply wagons to form part of a square, the open side facing the Smoky Hill and a copse of stunted willows. Somewhere in the bottoms a mule bawled from the remuda.

Miles looked toward the herd, a great patch of darkness on the lighter ground beyond the river. They would likely move out before dawn, heading for the Republican. He swung down from the tired bay and led it toward the Studebakers. A startling sound reached him, and he stopped short. A woman had laughed from within the wagon square,

17

and the sound of it drove a shaft of loneliness into him that touched the deep well of his sorrow. Ruth, his girl wife, had laughed like that. Shortly after the war, fever had stilled her laughter forever. The sound of woman's laughter now haunted him.

"Stop wheah yuh are," a harsh voice said in the darkness.

Miles looked toward the tall man who detached himself from the shadows of one of the wagons and moved quickly toward Miles. "I wasn't moving," said Miles.

The tall man grounded a long-barreled rifle. "Yuh ride late," he said.

"I was looking for some of my boys," said Miles. "Maybe you heard what happened to them? You Texans made a clean sweep."

"Cotton said yuh had a loose mouth." The Texan spat to one side. "Yuh keep talkin' like thet, mistah, and mebbe you'll have a comeuppance with some of us boys."

"A pleasure," said Miles. "I'll put you on the list."

"The name is Starr. Cass Starr."

The challenge hung in the quiet air. Miles looked steadily at the tall man.

"Yuh ridin' along to the Bozeman with us, mistah?" said Starr.

"I'm not sure," said Miles.

The Texan shifted his rifle. "I'm mebbe lookin' forward to it."

Miles led the bay on. He looked back. "How many men with this corrida?"

"Thirty."

"How many Texans?"

"Twenty."

Miles smiled. "Fair odds for one Yankee," he said.

Starr raised his head. "Why, gawddamn yuh!" he snapped.

"Is that you, Mister Flint?" Jonas Carlisle called out. His broad form was outlined against the firelight.

Miles could almost feel the savage hatred of the Texan behind him as he walked toward the trail driver. Nothing mattered at that moment to Miles Flint. There was a savagery within him, too, a cold, killing savagery that could only be sated by the blood of the man who had caused the destruction of his camp.

"We have saved some dinner for you, Mister Flint," said Jonas.

"I'll take care of my horse first," said Miles.

"A beautiful animal," said Carlisle. He lighted a cigar. "We thought you had left for Dodge."

18

Miles looked over his shoulder toward the west. "I had a hope that some of them might have survived."

"And now you do not."

Miles shook his head. He unsaddled the bay, rubbed him down, and then led him to the river, where he picketed him near the willows. Miles washed in the river. Now and then he heard the trail hands laughing around their fires near the chuckwagon, the center of any trail camp. It meant nothing to them that Miles's whole life had been blotted out in a matter of minutes because of their carelessness. Most of them had seen too much violent death to worry about the deaths of three Canucks and a nigger.

He picked up his rifle and walked toward the Studebakers. He saw Lorena before he entered the shifting circle of firelight. She was seated on a folding stool, dressed in a gingham dress almost like those worn by the gaunt emigrant women of the Oregon Trail, but there was a difference. This dress had likely not been sewed by her slim hands. It was fitted exquisitely to her form. Her dark hair had been swept up and fastened with a blood-red ribbon, and as she looked toward Miles the firelight sparkled from her dark eyes and deftly touched her full, soft lips with a red brush. She looked like a painting, except for the quick pulse in the hollow of her lovely throat, encircled with a black velvet ribbon held by a tiny diamond pin. It was almost as though she had been expecting him, knowing full well he would come . . . that he would *have* to come.

"A plate for Mister Flint, Pomp!" called out Jonas Carlisle. He looked at Miles. "Will you have whiskey, sir?"

"I can use it," said Miles.

"Bourbon or rye?"

Miles smiled. "Rye is a Westerner's drink," he said. He leaned his rifle against a wagon and hung his 'scope case from it.

Pomp, a small, fast-moving Negro with a tinge of gray in his dark wool, unfolded a table, deftly spread a cloth on it, placed *silverware,* not crude cutlery, on the cloth, set a filled plate on the table, then vanished again, only to reappear with the glass of rye. "Coffee, suh?" he said.

"Later, please, Pomp," said Miles.

Carlisle paced back and forth, sucking on his cigar, as though eager to have Miles finish his meal so that he could talk with him. Now and again he walked down toward the river, locked his arms behind his broad back, and stared thoughtfully to the north, where the ice-chip stars stippled the dark sky. It was then that Miles would raise his head to see Lorena looking directly at him, and her eyes did not shift when he looked deep into them. Yet she wasn't bold or wanton. How many men had she looked at that way?

"Why do you hunt buffalo, Mistah Flint?" she asked at last.

He looked up at her. "It's a living," he said.

"It's more than just that, isn't it?"

He nodded. "I'm my own boss. This is good country. A man is not penned within four walls. The wind and the sky are walls and roof enough for any man."

"Not *any* man," she said.

He looked at her and then away. It was disquieting, and yet he knew she was no bitch in heat.

"How many buffalo have you killed?" she asked as she accepted a cup of coffee from Pomp.

"I have never kept count, Mrs. Carlisle. I have averaged about twenty to forty a day for weeks on end, four years in all."

"And you intend to keep on?"

He nodded. "I want no other life. Not right now, at least."

"Jonas says you buffalo runners will kill yourselves out of business."

Miles shrugged. "It's inevitable. If I don't kill them, someone else will."

"And then what happens?"

He placed knife and fork on his plate and pushed it back. He drained his glass and felt for a cigar.

"Pomp!" said Jonas from behind Miles. "A cigar for Mister Flint!"

The little Negro appeared like the genie out of the legendary lantern, cigar box opened, a flint lighter in his other hand. Miles selected a long nine, and Pomp lighted it, then vanished.

Jonas sat down and placed heavy hands on his thighs. "You said Red Cloud would stand in the way. Did you mean that?"

Miles blew a smoke ring. "He does," he said dryly.

Spurs chimed softly and musically from behind Miles. "Indians," said a flat, toneless voice. "All they evah do is beg for sugah, tobacco, whiskey, and a wo-haw or two. A taste of powdersmoke will drive them off like gnats befo' a smudge fiah."

Miles turned slowly to see a man, perhaps half a head shorter than himself but every bit as broad-shouldered and muscular, standing in the opening between two of the wagons. There wasn't an ounce of fat on his tough frame, although he had six to seven years of age on Miles. There was a cold grayness about the man, from dusty gray hat to dark hair shot with gray at the sides to gray eyes almost disfiguring in their lightness against the darkness of his skin and thick dragoon mustache. This was a man who expected nothing but hardship and violence in his life. A fighting man from the looks of him, and the weak be damned.

Jonas stood up. "Beck, this gentleman is Miles Flint, the buffalo runner whose camp we inadvertently destroyed this afternoon. Mister Flint, this gentleman is Beckwith Sterret, my trail boss." There was a note of pride in Carlisle's voice as he mentioned Sterret.

Miles took the cigar from his mouth and stood up to face the trail boss. "I didn't find any of my men, Mister Sterret," he said quietly. He made no effort to extend a hand, nor did Sterret make a move to offer his. There was a coldness between them, perhaps a faint prophecy of death in the future.

Sterret rubbed his dusty jaw. "Three or fo' thousand buffalo and several hundred stampedin' longhorns don't let much stand in the way, Mistah Flint," said Sterret. There was no note of apology in his flat, even voice. No sorrow. Nothing of pity, of remorse, not even superficially, for the four men who had died because of his carelessness. Yet it was somehow just what Miles had expected.

"Those buffalo wouldn't have stampeded if you had diverted the herd in time," said Miles.

"We were on the way to watah, Mistah Flint," said the Texan. "We made twenty-five waterless miles today."

"And those cows couldn't wait another half hour by diversion past the buffalo," said Miles coldly.

Sterret raised his head. "It's my job to handle the herd," he said as though that excused everything else.

Miles nodded. "How many beeves did *you* lose, Mister Sterret?"

"Not a dam' one, Mistah Flint." He looked at Lorena. "Beggin' yore pardon, ma'am."

"I thought as much," said Miles.

For a moment they stood there studying each other, then Sterret looked at Jonas. "Herd is well bedded, Mistah Carlisle," he said as though nothing had happened between him and Miles. "I kep' the stampeded bunch this side of the river. We can cross them in the mornin'. I don't want the rest of the herd to be disturbed by them plowin' acrost the river."

"Fine," said Jonas. "Whiskey, Beck?"

"Don't mind if I do."

Miles sat down. Pomp had refilled his glass, and the little servant brought a glass to the trail boss. Sterret hunkered down on his heels and stared moodily into the fire, as though Miles

21

Flint had ceased to exist or at least to occupy his thoughts.

Jonas sat down. "Perhaps we can deal with Red Cloud, Mister Flint," he suggested.

Miles looked up from his rye. "Call me Miles," he said.

"Miles, then."

"I would be willing to deal with him," said Jonas thoughtfully.

"Deal, hell!" said Beck. "We can drive them like cattle."

"These are Teton Sioux," said Miles. "No one drives *them*."

"I thought Red Cloud was an Oglala," said Jonas.

"He is," said Miles. "The Teton Sioux is composed of the Oglalas, Baulés, Hunkpapas, Sans Arcs, Miniconjous, Wahpetons, and the Sihasapas. The Tetons form about half of the Sioux nation."

"Nation?" said Sterret. He spat to one side. "Yuh talk as if they were *white* men."

Jonas looked at his trail boss. "Please, Beck," he said. "Miles has had experience with these people. It may be of inestimable value to us."

Beck stood up and drained his glass. He looked sideways at Miles. "What did yuh have, Flint, a blanket dictionary?"

Jonas flushed. "Go check the night herders, Beck," he said.

"I'm the *trail boss*," said Sterret.

Jonas stood up slowly and looked at the Texan. Miles again caught the strength of Jonas Carlisle. A man used to authority and to giving orders.

Sterret pulled down the brim of his hat. "We pull out at first light," he said. He walked off, his spurs chiming softly.

Jonas sat down. "I apologize for him," he said. He narrowed his eyes as he saw the look on Miles's hawk face.

Miles sipped his liquor. "There is no need for that. I would not accept a personal apology from that man under any circumstances."

Lorena knew now why this lobo of a man had come into their camp, and it was not for food, warmth, or shelter. A cold feeling came over her, and she shivered in the night air.

"Get Mrs. Carlisle a shawl, Pomp," said Jonas. He looked at Miles. "Continue about the Sioux, if you please, sir."

Miles blew a smoke ring. "Red Cloud got riled during the war," he said. "Miners crossed into Montana from Idaho. Helena, Bozeman, and Virginia City sprang up like mushrooms. The Army wanted to build a road from Fort Laramie through the Powder River and Big Horn countries of Wyoming and then west across Montana as a shortcut from the East to the goldfields."

"The Bozeman Trail!" said Jonas.

"Exactly," said Miles.

22

"That is all Sioux coountry, is it not?" asked Lorena as Pomp draped the shawl about her shapely shoulders.

"They had driven the Crows from it," said Miles. He relighted his cigar and looked into the dying fire as though conjuring up the picture. "The Sioux and the Northern Cheyenne claimed the white man was frightening the buffalo. So they held the Powder River valley and the surrounding country, filled with buffalo, as an everlasting supply of meat and hides."

"They kill only what they need," she said.

Jonas looked at her. "They stand in the way," he said.

"It sounds so cruel, Jonas."

"It is progress," he said flatly.

Miles watched Pomp refill the rye glass. "Some Sioux chiefs signed a treaty for the new Army road. The Bozeman Trail. But they were only subchiefs. Red Cloud and many other chiefs did not sign. The Army went ahead anyway. Red Cloud captured some soldiers and civilian workers, held them prisoner for two weeks, and then released them because his young men had threatened to kill them." He looked at Jonas. "Red Cloud said, 'I shall stand in the trail.' "

"And is he?" said Lorena.

"Yes," said Miles.

"It is said that he came to Fort Laramie to deal with the Army," said Jonas.

"He did," said Miles. "The road was being built. Fort Reno had been built on the Powder River one hundred and seventy-five miles from Fort Laramie. Goldseekers were already pushing up the Bozeman Trail. Nothing could stop them. They had the 'white man's sickness,' according to the Sioux. We call it gold fever. Red Cloud would not sell his hunting grounds. The Army kept on anyway. They began to build Fort Phil Kearny fifty miles northwest of Fort Reno, on Piney Fork of Lodge Pole Creek in the Big Horn Mountains. Red Cloud began to gather his strength. Spotted Tail of the Brulés joined him with his warriors. About a hundred miles beyond Fort Kearny the Army built Fort C. F. Smith. Red Cloud countered by trying to enlist his bitter enemies, the Crows, against the whites in an all-out war. The Crows refused. But in time Fort Phil Kearny was virtually under siege. The Army had its fort, but it was useless—Red Cloud *had* barred the Bozeman."

"Nelson Story got through," said Lorena. "You were with him."

"God alone knows how we got through," said Miles. Memories flooded back to him. "The Army refused to let Story pass with his thousands of Texas cattle, a handful of Texans, and one lone Yankee." He smiled wryly. "With the luck of a genius, or a fool, whichever way one looks at it, Story got through to the Gallatin."

"My country," said Jonas.

"And the Bozeman Trail?" said Lorena.

Miles looked at her. Her loveliness struck him again. "The Army was forced to abandon the Big Horn country. Forts Smith, Kearny, and Reno were burned by the Indians while the retreating soldiers were still within sight of the smoke. It was a defeat for the Army. There are no soldiers in that country now. In exchange Red Cloud agreed to let the building of the Union Pacific go unchallenged. He has kept his word on that."

"And do you not think we can make it, Miles?" said Jonas.

"No," said Miles flatly. "Drive your herd back to the railhead and sell it. There is money in trail driving that way. All you'll find on the Bozeman Trail is death and the loss of everything. The time is not yet for trail herds to follow the way of Nelson Story."

The firelight played on Jonas's strong bearded face as he paced back and forth. There was no fear on his face. "Montana is my destiny," he said. "There the grass is knee-deep and the water plentiful and sweet. There are sheltered valleys along the Gallatin for thousands of head of good beeves. The government allowed me a great grant there for services rendered, and I plan to add more land to it. I mean to build an empire there, Miles."

"You'll have to get there first," said Miles dryly.

"I mean to." Jonas stopped pacing and looked directly at Miles. "You'll join us?"

"No."

Lorena shifted a little in her seat and adjusted her shawl. She shot a quick glance at Miles and then flushed a little as he saw her.

Miles stood up. "I can ride north for a time with you. The buffalo will be drifting north to get the cured grass. I can resupply at Fort Leavenworth."

Jonas smiled. "Thanks, Miles."

Miles bowed a little to Lorena. "Evenin', ma'am," he said.

She nodded her shapely head and watched the two men walk toward the river.

Jonas stopped at the edge of the river. "One thing, Miles, I must say. My men are Texans for the most part. Almost all of them are Confederate veterans. They are tough as rawhide and bowie steel. They obey me and work hard for me because I pay top wages and treat them squarely. They know I am of Yankee stock, but I give them no cause for quarrel on that account."

24

"The war is over," said Miles. "They lost. It's about time they faced the truth."

Jonas inspected the glowing end of his cigar. "These men are not to be trifled with. I have seen swift and killing gunplay for less than what passed between you and Cotton this afternoon, and Beck Sterret as well."

"I lost four friends out there today," said Miles.

"You cannot blame all of us for that."

"I can blame one man," said Miles.

Jonas nodded. "I see. It's like that, then."

"It's like that," repeated Miles.

"Good night," said Miles. He watched the trail driver walk toward the dying firelight. Lorena rose to meet him. He placed an arm around her slim waist and walked her to the nearest wagon and helped her in. He walked back to the fire, staring into the ash-covered embers.

Miles made his bunk. He pulled off his moccasins and sat there watching Jonas until the firelight was gone. A lamp flared up in the Studebaker where Lorena was. Miles saw the broad shadow of Jonas cast upon the tilt by the yellow light of the lantern. Then the lamp flicked out.

CHAPTER THREE

The smoke of the cookfire rose thin and threadlike against the first faint traces of dawn in the eastern sky, but already the air was thickening with dust as the smaller herd on the south bank was pushed across the shallow river, the "swimmers," or lead cows, splashing willingly into the cool water, eyes wide and staring, horns glistening wetly. The drivers had eaten in shifts while it was still dark. Already, across the Smoky Hill, the point riders were shaping up the herd, while the swing and flank riders were "crowding" the herd into the trail formation, with much shouting and popping of rawhide lashes.

The first mounts of the day had been selected from the remuda of over ninety horses, some of them half broken and all of them lively. The wrangler, helped by a few hands, had formed a fence of ropes between two supply wagons and had held the remuda there while each herder had selected his mount and roped it. Before the first true light of dawn exploded silently in the east, the herd was one unit again and the point was a good mile and a half up the trail, led by Old Brimstone, the ten-year-old steer who had an uncanny way of picking the best trail. Ernie Masland had told Miles over a cup of Arbuckle's best that Jonas Carlisle had paid aplenty for Old Brimstone back in Texas.

Miles saddled his bay as the wagons rolled toward the ford. Float logs were lashed along the sides but proved to be unnecessary, for the water hardly rose above the level of the wagon beds. The remuda splashed past, driven by the wrangler and his helper, the two youngest hands in the Carlisle corrida. The dust rose thickly from the trail to meet the light of the dawn. Miles slung his cased 'scope and heavy Sharps to the saddle and then lighted a cigar, watching the smooth efficiency of the corrida, ramrodded by Beck Sterret, who had been up before the cocinero. The man missed nothing.

Two horses were ground-reined near the last of the Studebakers. Jonas Carlisle walked to one of them and turned to give Lorena a hand into the sidesaddle, arranging her riding habit skirt so that it fell in full folds, revealing only the tips of her tiny riding boots. He reached up and patted her face, then mounted himself and rode toward Miles.

Miles mounted and waited for the trail driver.

Jonas drew rein. "Where will you ride today?" he asked.

Miles shrugged. *"Quien sabe?* Out of the dust. I thought perhaps antelope steaks would go good tonight."

Jonas smiled. "Capital!" He placed a hand on his cantle roll and looked back at Lorena. "Keep her company for a while, like a good fellow." He touched his horse with his spurs and rode into the river, his eyes on his valued herd and not on his valued wife. The thought was that of Miles Flint.

The dawn wind was whipping her riding-habit skirts and her dark hair as he rode toward her. She placed a little gloved hand against her hair and hastily adjusted it with hairpins, a gesture so utterly feminine and concentrated that it brought another pang of piercing memory to Miles.

"Are you riding with me, Miles?" she said.

"I had hoped to."

She smiled quickly. "It does get lonely," she said. "I can't stand to ride in those wagons."

"We can cross upstream. There is another ford there, and the dust is downwind."

They rode knee to knee toward the ford. Miles entered the water first to test the depth, then beckoned to her. Her mare splashed into the water. The two horses struggled out on the far bank. The herd was still there, coming into clear view in the gathering light of the day. The two "point" riders con-

26

trolled the lead, with the upwind side handled by Cass Starr, the *segundo*, second-in-command to the trail boss. Along the sides of the strung-out herd were first the "swing" and then the "flank" riders, with the "drag" riders closing up the rear, eating dust, gathering in the strays, driving on the stragglers. The remuda trotted along upwind of the herd, with the wagons upwind of them. Already the chuckwagon was gaining on the rest of the wagons, so that the cocinero could have coffee and cold fare ready at the noon halt. The whole formation was efficient and safe enough in Kansas, but along the Bozeman they'd have to tighten up or Jonas would find painted warriors cutting in on his horses, wagons, cattle, and perhaps even his woman.

The sun flared up, touching the prairie with golden light, changing the dull pewter of the Smoky Hill into a quick burst of silver, glinting from the wet hides of the cattle that had crossed the river that morning and reflecting from the polished horns of the herd.

"Where did you meet Nelson Story?" asked Lorena.

Miles looked at her with a start. He had been preoccupied with the drive and the coming of the summer day. "Fort Laramie," he said.

"Were you a soldier then?"

"No, but I had been scouting the Powder River country for the Army."

"Why did Nelson Story drive to Montana?" she asked.

"He had made a strike on a placer claim near Summit, at the head of Alder Gulch, or what is now Virginia City. He knew he could make a killing by trail driving north from Texas to Missouri, now that he had capital. With one companion he rode from Virginia City right through the Sioux country with forty thousand dollars in his jeans. He bought his beef in Texas and drove it north toward Missouri, but the Kansas Jayhawkers wanted two dollars a head toll. Thousands of head of cattle were backed up near Baxter Springs because the Texas trail drivers had cattle aplenty and no money at all. Those who tried to drive through met death and defeat. More than a quarter of a million steers were backed up south of the Missouri line when Story got there."

She looked at him. "And that was when he decided to try for Montana?"

Miles nodded. "He had already driven his herd of three thousand head five hundred miles. He knew Montana could use beef on the hoof. So he pointed his herd west and then north, aiming for Montana, twenty-one hundred miles away and right through the heart of the Sioux country."

"So you rode with him."

27

He grinned. "I could hardly let one Yankee take the chances he was taking."

"Against the Sioux?"

He grinned again. "No, against the Texans who were riding with him."

"That isn't fair!" she cried.

"I won't apologize," he said.

"But how did you get through the Sioux country?"

"God only knows. We could have cut southwest from Fort Laramie to the Oregon Trail, then over the divide into Idaho, then recrossing north into Virginia City. But it meant crossing two high mountain passes. The season was getting on. The passes might be blocked with snow. The Bozeman Trail, dangerous as it was, was lower and about two hundred and fifty miles shorter. We pointed them north, Mrs. Carlisle."

"Please call me Lorena," she said.

He looked into those eyes, and his senses seemed to swim a little. "Lorena, then," he said quietly.

"When did you see the Indians, Miles?"

"Oh, they were always around, although we saw them only when they wanted to be seen." He would not mention the charred areas they had passed along the Bozeman, with rust-scaled wagon iron lying in thick ashes and other more gruesome things lying about. She would likely see them soon enough if Jonas Carlisle had his way.

The sun rose higher, fashioning the dry heat of the day. The sky was as yet cloudless, stained only by the thick trail dust that rose high to be tattered by the wind.

"We taught the Sioux a lesson with the rolling-block, breech-loading Remington rifles Nelson Story had bought at Fort Leavenworth," continued Miles. "They couldn't figure out how we could shoot and reload so fast—they only knew about the muzzle-loading rifles still used by the Army. They got a few nasty surprises." He would not mention the two herders who had been cut off and found later where they had fallen, pincushioned with arrows, scalped and mutilated, with their genitals stuffed into their tongueless mouths. "We got to Fort Phil Kearny without too much trouble. It was virtually under siege. They had all they could do to protect themselves, much less supply escort for two mad Yankees and a passel of sun-burned Texans, ex-rebels to a man, talking like they actually *meant* to drive three thousand longhorns to the Gallatin."

"And they did!" said Lorena proudly.

"Led by a Yankee," said Miles dryly. He couldn't help it. "We actually had to sneak away from Fort Kearny because the commanding officer had forbidden us to go on. We knew that if we stayed there it would only be a matter of time before

28

the Sioux had run off all our horses and cattle. They had already picked off one night herder."

"What happened to him, Miles?"

He looked away. "They killed him." There was no use in itemizing what they had done to him *before he had died*. Even now the memory made Miles a little queasy. "We moved north every night, for the Sioux do not fight at night. We left the Powder River country for the Tongue River. It was late in the season. October was almost gone. The Sioux had closed in behind us. There was no going back. Six weeks later the Sioux wiped out eighty troopers under Captain Fetterman almost within sight of Fort Kearny. We herded during the day, holding off the Sioux raids, then drove at night. We turned west toward the Big Horn and crossed it just about where the Army later built Fort C. F. Smith, which the Sioux burned a few years later after it was abandoned. We headed for the Yellowstone, with the Remingtons hardly ever cooling off. They made one last attack and got beaten. After that there was nothing to it. We forded the Yellowstone, passed through Emigrant Gulch, reached the town of Bozeman, and turned the cattle loose in the valley of the Gallatin. That's all there was to it."

"Just like thet," she said.

"It does sound heroic," he admitted.

"Wasn't it, Miles?"

He shifted in his saddle. "It was a job," he said. "Someone else would have done it if we hadn't."

"I wonder," she said. She looked at him. "Miles, what do they do to white women if they capture them?"

He could not lie to her, nor could he tell her the truth. To be "passed on the prairie" was worse, far worse than sudden death. Stripped naked, spread-eagled on the harsh earth, seeing with horror-stricken eyes the long line of bucks waiting their turn until constant and savage rape brought death the long, slow, agonizing way. Miles had helped bury the pitiful, bloody, broken remnants of such atrocities and had been haunted for months afterward by the memories of them. One girl had been but twelve years old and still alive when they had found her, screaming and staring at them with eyes that held no sense in them.

"Miles?" she said.

He shifted in his saddle. "Ask your husband," he said almost brutally. And why not? It was Jonas Carlisle who was taking her, along with rest of his possessions, up the bloody, dangerous Bozeman Trail. Let *him* answer.

She did not ask again. All that morning, until they saw the wind-blown thread of smoke from the noon campfire, they

29

spoke of many things, but never of what was in each of their minds. Miles thought it must seem obvious to her how he felt.

A cup of steaming Arbuckle's and a good cigar from the store of Jonas Carlisle were enough for Miles at noon. He went on ahead long before the herd moved out. One of the herders had said he had seen antelope on a ridge far ahead, moving away from the oncoming herd.

Lorena Carlisle watched the broad, buckskinned back of the hunter as he rode north from the camp. Thin dust arose from his bay's hoofs and hung about Miles, lending an almost unreal quality to the scene. She looked away for a moment and he was gone, as though cleanly wiped from the landscape by the turpentined rag of an artist impatient with his mistake. There was something disquieting about Miles Flint. He had appeared out of nowhere, almost as though his buffalo hunting had been nothing but a device to while away the time until the trail herd reached the Smoky Hill country. But why had he come? What did he really want? What would he take with him? For she knew, as surely as she stood there, watching the dust of his passage drift away, that Miles Flint would not leave without taking *something* with him.

The late-afternoon sun slanted down on the yellowed grasses. A vagrant wind rippled the grass until it looked like waves washing toward some far and unseen shore. A low line of hills shimmering in the heat marked the line of a distant creek, stippled by cottonwoods and willows. To the south rose a thin wraith of dust that marked the steady approach of the trail herd toward the night camp on the creek. Already, somewhere between Miles and the trail herd, the trail boss or one of his best men would be scouting the trail toward the water.

Miles rested his chin on his crossed wrists, studying the antelope upwind of him. The antelope had moved all that afternoon ahead of the herd, putting plenty of distance between themselves and the cattle. They were not too concerned about the herd. Their incredible eyesight and keen scent were enough to alert them in plenty of time if danger approached. What they did *not* see or sense was the bareheaded man lying at the lip of a buffalo wallow, his head concealed in a clump of scant soapweed, who had been watching them for some time through a pair of binoculars shaded with his dusty hat so that the bright sunlight would not reflect from the polished lenses.

Miles eased up his Sharps and rested it on the lip of the wallow. The wind was constantly fishtailing, and the heat waves shimmered up from the dry earth and made the pronghorns look at times as though they were actually grazing several feet from the ground. Miles fullcocked the rifle's heavy outside hammer and nestled a shoulder against its brass butt-plate. The nearest buck was a good two hundred and seventy-five yards away, half hidden in another wallow, his head moving up and down as he grazed. Miles looked back over his shoulder. He didn't want to startle the tired herd with the heavy report of the rifle, and yet he couldn't get any closer to the pronghorns without being seen.

Miles drew in a deep breath and let half of it out. He closed his right hand around the small of the stock and touched the trigger with the first joint of his trigger finger. He took up the slack as the 'scope crosshairs settled on the pronghorn. The antelope seemed to swim into view. For a moment he stood there seemingly looking directly at Miles; then he moved, contracting the muscles on his smooth rump. A white patch appeared on the rump, almost as though someone had thrown a switch. The patch alerted the herd, but before the antelope sprang off the Sharps flashed and roared, and the buck was flung lifelessly into the hollow with half of its head missing. The booming echo of the shot fled across the rolling ground and echoed faintly from the distant line of hills.

"Excellent shooting," said a voice behind Miles.

Miles turned quickly to see Jonas Carlisle sitting on his blocky gray horse beside that of Beck Sterret.

Sterret spat sideways. "A man oughta use open sights," he said. "Ain't hardly fair to a beast to get killed through a sightin' pipe like thet."

Miles stood up and snapped the 'scope loose. He placed it on the ground and reloaded the Sharps. He looked toward the pronghorns. Most of them were out of sight, bounding across the yellowed grasses like blown leaves before the autumn wind, but a smaller group had broken loose from the herd to streak south instead of west. Miles flipped up the rear sight of the Sharps and raised the rifle. He adjusted the rear-sight slide and sighted through the V notch, centering the brass-blade front sight. He fired almost the instant the sights settled on a young buck. The buck rolled rump over head, and where the white patch had been on his rump there was a spreading stain of red. The echo of the shot died away, and the powder-smoke drifted on the wind.

Miles picked up the 'scope and placed it in its case. He ejected the brass hull and reloaded the rifle. He carried the Sharps to the bay and placed the rifle in its slings. He picked up his hat and placed it on his head, then cased his binoculars.

31

"I'll pick up the meat, Mister Carlisle," he said. He swung up on the bay and rode toward the dead antelopes.

Jonas Carlisle relighted his cigar and looked at Beck Sterret. "What have you to say now?" he said.

Beck began to fashion a smoke. "Luck," he said.

"Not hardly," said Jonas.

Beck passed his tongue along the cigarette paper. "I wonder how good he is with a six-shooter?"

Jonas looked back toward the approaching herd. "Why trouble to find out?" he said quietly. "Get this straight, Beck. I want no trouble between you and that man. I need him. He knows the Bozeman Trail and the ways of the Sioux. With that rifle in his hands he could hold off fifty of them and never raise a sweat. We *need* him. I repeat . . . we *need* him. Remember that!"

Beck snapped a lucifer on his thumbnail and lighted the quirly. He looked after Miles and idly fanned out the match. "How *long* we goin' to need him, Mistah Carlisle?" he said.

"Until we reach the Gallatin, Beck."

Beck nodded. "I'll wait until then."

Jonas turned. His face was set. "One more thing, Beck, as long as we're on the subject. I've heard talk amongst your Texas boys about this man. Cotton, as usual, is shooting off his big mouth, and Cass Starr has been doing a lot of talking, too. You've got a score of Texans thinking the same way you do."

Beck blew a smoke ring. "I can't tell them how to think, Boss."

Jonas reached out a heavy hand and pointed a thick finger at Beck. "No, you can't, but you *can* keep control of their actions. It means their jobs if they go out of their way to rile this man."

Beck grinned. "Yore talkin' like a man protectin' a child, Mistah Carlisle."

Jonas lowered his hand. "Then I'll give it to you straight. I hired you as trail boss and paid you extra wages, with an assured bonus if we get through to the Gallatin, because you're the best in the business. So far you have proven that. Your job is to handle this herd and handle the men who are working for me. It is also your job to prevent trouble *and* bloodshed. Do you follow me?"

Beck nodded sourly. "I follow you, Mistah Carlisle. I can personally wait until we reach the Gallatin."

Jonas kneed his horse away and rode toward the approaching herd. He looked back at Beck. "Don't underestimate that man, Beck. Have you ever seen rifle shooting like that?"

Beck blew another smoke ring. He looked back at Miles,

now dismounted near one of the dead pronghorns. "Yeh," he said thoughtfully. "But thet was a long ways from heah, Mistah Carlisle. Place named Gettysburg."

Miles had both antelope skinned, gutted, and hung up to cool before the first longhorns topped a nearby ridge and smelled the water of the creek. They bellowed and lowed as they streamed down toward the creek, guided by the cursing point riders who headed them downstream from the willows and cottonwoods where Miles had picked the campsite. The chuckwagon topped the ridge and swayed down the slope toward Miles, skillfully driven by Ernie Masland, the cocinero.

While Miles rubbed down the bay Masland set up his office. In no time at all he had a fire going, started from the stock of chips he carried in the "cooney" or "possum belly," a hide slung beneath the wagon body. By the time Miles had finished with the bay and had picketed him upstream in a grassy swale he could smell the mingled odors of the burning buffalo chips and coffee brewing. He carried his rifle to the chuckwagon and was honored with a mug of coffee.

Pomp was setting up Carlisle's camp aided by the drivers of the other Studebakers. Lorena was seated in the shade of one of the wagons, and now and then Miles caught her looking toward the chuckwagon.

Ernie filled a cup for himself and squatted beside the fire. "Thanks again for the meat," he said.

"Por nada," said Miles.

Ernie looked sideways at Miles. "I think I better warn yuh, Miles. Some of these Lone Star boys ain't forgot there was a war a few years back. They don't cater much to Yankees. Beck Sterret fit with Hood's Texans all through the war. Yuh can't get 'em much tougher and meaner than them."

Miles nodded. "I met a few of them."

"You was in the war yourself?"

Miles nodded. "Four years."

"But you was a bluebelly?"

"Yes."

Ernie grinned. "Ain't a one of 'em in the camp outside of me. I fit with the Eighth Kansas. First Brigade, Third Division, Fourth Corps, Army of the Cumberland."

"You've got a good memory," said Miles. "You were telling about these Texas boys."

Ernie drained his cup. "Well, they don't bother me none and they better not. Mister Carlisle hired me because I'm the best cocinero in the business. These boys want to eat right and on time, they don't fool with good ol' Ern, I tell yuh."

"You're an artist," admitted Miles.

Ernie waved a hand in casual acceptance of the God's hon-

33

est truth. "Oh, I allow as how yuh can handle yoreself with most of these boys. Some of these Texicans is all belt buckle and mouth, but not all of 'em. Cotton is a killer, for all his big mouth. Cass Starr is as rough as a cob. Both are fast men with a gun. The one yuh should watch is the quietest of the lot."

"Who?" said Miles.

Ernie looked toward where the herd was being watered. The strident voice of Beck Sterret rose above the clamor. "Him," he said.

"He's fast?" said Miles.

Ernie nodded. "I've seen him. Faster than thunder and eleven claps of lightnin'. Don't let them gray hairs fool yuh, Miles. He's good. And he don't like you one damned little bit."

Miles stood up. "The feeling is more than mutual."

"Whatever the hell that means." Ernie stood up. "Got to get grub started. The first shift will be along soon. You ridin' to the Gallatin with us?"

"Quien sabe?"

"Well, if I was you, I'd keep away from Beck Sterret. He ramrods this corrida, and I mean *ramrods*. Keep away from him and he won't likely bother yuh. I'd like to see yuh make the whole drive, but for yore own good I'd rather see you leave."

Miles looked toward the herd. "Thanks," he said quietly. "But if I do ride to the Gallatin, maybe you'd better worry a little about Beck Sterret, too, along with worrying about me. I can wait until we reach the Gallatin to finish my business."

Ernie had a puzzled look on his homely face. "Meanin' what?"

Miles walked a few paces and then looked back. "I mean four dead men on the fork of the Smoky Hill." He walked on and did not look back.

Ernie felt a cold shiver of fear work through him. "Jesus God," he said. "I never figgered it thataway."

CHAPTER FOUR

There was a faint touch of moonlight in the eastern sky when Miles finished cleaning his Sharps. He carried the heavy rifle with him to the chuckwagon and leaned it against a front wheel. Ernie Masland ladled food onto a tin plate and filled a cup of coffee. A dozen or so of the trail drivers lay on their sides, propped on an elbow or squatted on their feet beside the fire, the light striking the hard planes of their brown faces. They were talking in low voices, and now and then a ripple of laughter broke out. Ernie placed Miles's plate and cup on the folded-down shelf at the rear of the chuckwagon, a high honor indeed for any member of a trail drive.

Someone came up quietly behind Miles. He turned to see the shining black face of Pomp.

"Mistuh Carlisle says you is to eat with him tonight, suh," said the little Negro.

"My apologies to Mister Carlisle," said Miles. "I have already been served here."

Brown faces turned to watch Miles and the Negro. They were absolutely expressionless.

Pomp looked puzzled. "Mistuh Carlisle might not like that, suh. Beggin' your pardon, suh."

Miles smiled. "I'll talk to him later, Pomp."

"Yessuh," said Pomp. He trotted back to the Studebakers. Miles saw the glow of the firelight on the silverware and the snow-white napery. This drive was a *little* different from that of Nelson Story, for that he-coon of a man had quite often eaten his beans and bacon with his fingers, with the rain running from the brim of his hat into the tin plate, joking with his drivers.

"Don't yuh like hobnobbin' with society, Flint?" drawled one of the drivers.

"Hell's fire, Flint ain't one of *us* boys," said another. "Flint is a *hunter*. Them's big apples out heah."

Ernie shot a warning glance at Miles. "Mebbe yuh shoulda gone," he said out of the side of his mouth. "The boys is lookin' for a little fun."

Miles speared a bit of steak and popped it into his mouth.

35

"Prime," he said with a sideways tilt of his head. "I'm no social light, Ernie. I agreed to ride with the drive for a time. I'm under no obligation to wield silverware and make with polite conversation. I did my job today. That's all that's required of me."

A rider came pounding through the darkness and flung off near the fire. His spurs rang sharply as he walked to the fire. "Beck wants yuh out theah, Ben," he said. "Pronto!"

"Goin', Cotton," said the lean driver. He placed cup and plate in the big tin basin, belched politely, and fashioned a smoke as he walked toward his horse.

Cotton glanced toward Miles. "Got a plate, Ern?" he said. "Beck is comin' in."

"Do tell," said Ern. "I thought he was goin' to sleep out there with them cows all night."

Cotton rolled a smoke, watching Miles all the while. His gaze drifted toward the big Sharps rifle. He lighted the quirly and sauntered over toward the rifle. Quickly he picked it up and hefted it.

"What yuh aim to do with thet smokepole, Cotton?" said a driver.

Cotton looked at him. "Ain't made up my mind, Vance," he said. He did not look at Miles. None of them did.

Cotton pulled off the fitted leather eyepies of the 'scope and peered curiously through them. The muzzle swung directly on Miles. "Heavy sonofabitch," said Cotton. "Wouldn't be much of a saddle gun, Like to bust a hosse's back."

Ernie looked at Cotton. "It ain't used in the saddle, Cotton," he said. "Most buffler hunters work afoot."

Cotton hefted the rifle. "Figgers," he said thoughtfully. "But the Yankees was nevah any great shakes durin' the wah on hossback anyways."

Miles placed his empty cup on the shelf. "How would you know, Cotton?" he said quietly.

The shot went home. The lean Texan went pale beneath his tan. His knuckles whitened as he gripped the rifle.

One of the men at the fire laughed softly and looked up at Cotton. "He's got yuh theah, Cotton," he said.

Cotton turned sharply. "You keep yore mouth shut, Jonce," he said harshly.

Jonce flushed. He was a good ten years older than Cotton. "I don't take ordehs from you, Cotton," he said.

Cotton stared at him, and it was then that Miles saw something in the young Texan's eyes—a wild, killing look. The barrel of the rifle rang against the tire iron as Cotton slammed the rifle butt on the ground.

"Careful!" snapped Miles.

Cotton tore his wild look from Jonce and looked at Miles, and now his tanned face was forcibly composed, his eyes cold, his lean hands hanging by his sides. "Yuh talkin' to me?" he said.

"I am," said Miles levelly.

The cold blue eyes stared unblinkingly at Miles. "I won't hurt yore gawddam' shootin' iron," he said. His glance flicked down to Miles's holstered Remington.

The challenge was there, ready to be tripped by the trigger sear of Miles's temper. "Let the rifle alone, Cotton," said Miles quietly. "You've had your fun."

Spurs jingled and leather creaked as man after man at the fire stood up and walked from behind Miles. It was suddenly very quiet around the chuckwagon. The distant sound of the restless herd drifted to them, mingled with the murmur of the creek and the soft sigh of the dry wind. The firelight reflected from the eyes of the men and the brass trim of their pistol butts.

Cotton extended his left hand and rested it on the barrel of the Sharps.

"Let the rifle alone," said Miles.

Cotton smiled quickly. "Shore, shore," he said. He gave an almost imperceptible push to the rifle. It fell heavily, clanging against the ironbound hub of the heavy wheel.

"Damn you!" snapped Miles. He walked toward Cotton.

Hoofbeats sounded behind Miles, but he did not turn. A man's boots struck the hard ground, and spurs chimed softly.

"Yuh talkin' to me thet way, Yankee?" drawled Cotton softly.

The die was set. A fraction of a second would tell the tale.

"Pick up thet rifle, Cotton," the quiet voice said from behind Miles.

Cotton stared past Miles with that unblinking look. "I don't take no ordehs from a gawddam' Yankee, Beck!" he snapped.

"You'll take ordehs from *me*, Cotton," said the trail boss.

It was quieter than it had been before, or so it seemed to Miles. There was a scuffling sound and the ringing of spurs as the drivers moved once again. This was a different matter. One Texan against another. An old hand against a comer maybe as fast as John Wesley Hardin, or so some said. But Beck Sterret had once faced down Ben Thompson in Fort Worth.

Cotton shifted on his feet, but his right hand was still hovering over his pistol butt, while he divided his attention between Miles and Beck.

"Pick up thet rifle," repeated Beck. "I won't tell yuh again, Cotton."

Cotton hesitated. God how he hated to back down in front

37

of this Yankee upstart! He glanced swiftly at Beck, and although Miles could not see Beck's face, he knew what was written on it. Cotton could put up or shut up. It was as simple as that. The fight was out of Miles's hands now. It no longer dealt with the rifle and the hazing of a Yankee by a troublemaking Texan.

Spurs chimed softly as Beck shifted.

Cotton took his lower lip between his even white teeth. He knelt slowly and picked up the Sharps. He placed it as he had found it. His eyes flicked toward Miles, and there was pure hell in them.

"Yuh wasn't told to come heah and hang around, Cotton," said Beck. "I sent yuh for Ben."

"I got him," said Cotton sullenly.

"Yore still on first night shift," said Beck.

Cotton took a deep breath. "All right, Beck," he said. He stalked to his horse and swung up into the saddle with a smashing of leather, wheeled the horse, set the cruel Mex spurs he favored into the quivering flanks of the horse, and shot out of the camp, missing some of the men near the fire by inches.

"Loco bastahd," said Jonce. "He'll kill thet hoss one of these days."

Cass Starr lounged into the glow of the firelight and glanced casually toward Miles. "He'll shore as hell kill somethin'," he drawled.

Miles looked at Beck Sterret. *"Gracias,"* he said.

Beck's eyes were as cold as Cotton's had been, but there was no killing look in them, just utter dislike. "Yuh rile him into thet exhibition?" he asked.

"No, he didn't, Beck," said Ernie Masland.

"I didn't ask you," said Beck coldly.

Miles shook his head.

Beck nodded. "Yuh got to remember these boys is Texans for the most part," he said. "They ain't forgot the wah."

"Cotton evidently wasn't in it," said Miles.

"His pappy was killed at Sharpsburg. His oldest brothah died of fever at Manassas. The next brothah died alongside of me at Gettysburg." He narrowed his eyes. "Near Little Round Top."

"Interesting," said Miles.

Beck shifted a little. "I got a job to do heah, Flint. I aim to do it. One way or anothah. I'd give you what I gave him, if you was to get out of hand on this drive."

"So? I'm not working for *you*, Sterret."

Beck looked beyond Miles, toward the unseen herd, and it seemed as though he was looking far beyond the herd, toward the Saline, the Solomon, the Prairie Dog, and Sappa Greek to the forks of the Republican and beyond, to the North Platte, Rush Creek and Pumpkin Creek, and the Laramie, thence north to the Powder and the Crazy Woman, the Big Horn and the Yellowstone, to the far-distant Gallatin.

Beck Sterret seemed to tear his gaze away from the known, but unseen. He looked at Miles, almost like a sleepwalker. "As long as yuh ride with us, Flint," he said quietly, "yore part of this drive, and don't yuh ever forget it. Yuh come up to measurement or yuh go. *One way or anothah, Flint, yuh go . . .*" Beck turned on a heel, walked to his horse, swung up into the saddle, and rode off toward the herd.

Miles refilled his coffee cup. "Nice fella," he observed to Ernie Masland.

"He didn't interfere there for love of you, that's for certain," said Ernie. He looked off into the darkness. "But, by God, man for man, Texan for Texan, he's the best trail boss in the business."

"Amen," said Miles. He drained his cup and walked to his rifle, inspecting it carefully, running a sleeve over the dusty barrel, under the amused eyes of the drivers who were back in squatting position about the dying fire. None of them said anything . . . maybe not just out of respect for Beck Sterret's orders, but because the tall, gray-eyed Yankee hadn't backed down before Cotton—or Beck Sterret, for that matter. That was a thoughtful cud for a man to chew.

Miles walked to his hotroll, flung on the ground beside the willows not far from the creek edge. He leaned his rifle against a tree and lighted a cigar. He dropped atop his hotroll, locked his hands at the nape of his neck, and studied the winking stars. It had been a nigh thing between him and Cotton. Miles was no leather-slapper, although he was no slouch on the draw. He knew well enough these Texans were teethed on six-shooters, and the worst of them was usually better than other men, non-Texans, with the exception of the Yankee gunfighters, marshals of such peaceful places as Wichita, Dodge City, and Abilene, called by the Texas trail drivers, half with sarcasm and half with respect, "The Fighting Pimps," because they seemed to spend most of their time, when not enforcing the law, with the painted ladies and calico cats of the bordellos.

Jonas Carlisle rode past in the semidarkness beyond the willows. He spent almost as much time with the herd as Beck Sterret did. Miles rolled over on his side. Lorena Carlisle was seated by the fire, its glow reflecting from her lovely face. Even as Miles looked toward her, she looked directly at him, although she could not see him beyond the pool of flickering

39

firelight; he had the uncanny feeling that she was bridging the gap between them and that she *knew* he was looking at her.

Miles looked the other way. It was disquieting to have her so near and yet the property of another man, a man whom Miles respected and liked. He must have dozed off, for suddenly he was alerted, rolling over on his other side, hand gripping pistol butt, the unlighted cigar dropping from his mouth. He drew and cocked the Remington in one fluid motion.

"Land o' Goshen, Mistuh 'Flint!" quavered Pomp. "It's only me! Pomp! Y'all move like a cat. Mistuh Flint! Please put down that gun! It's only Pomp, I tell you!"

Miles grinned. He let down the pistol hammer. "Don't ever walk up on a man like that in this country, Pomp," he said.

"I on'y come to tell you that Mis' Carlisle wants you to have coffee with her."

Miles sat up and sheathed the Remington. He glanced toward the fire. She was still sitting there. There was no sign of her husband. Miles hesitated. He had avoided having dinner with them. He did not want to expose himself to Lorena Carlisle any more than he had to, and yet he knew he'd have to go. "Tell her I'll be right along, Pomp," he said.

He washed up at the creek's edge. The moon cast a cool glow down the center of the dark waters. The wind had died down a little, rustling the leaves and sighing through the trees. Miles walked toward the campfire. She looked up as she heard him, and the look on her face drove into his heart like a Comanche lance. He knew he should not have come, and yet he knew he could not have stayed away.

"I hoped you would come, Miles," she said.

He took off his hat. "Hunting is a lonely life," he said, "and most of these drivers are not exactly sociable with me."

"Perhaps they have not forgotten the wah," she said.

He sat down and looked at her. "They were not the only ones who suffered," he said. "My brother died in Andersonville. Seventeen years old. My best friend died at Fredericksburg. I have done my best to forget the war."

"The No'th won," she said dryly.

He looked over his shoulder. "Montana is neither North nor South, and by that I do not mean geographically. Many of these men may stay there and become Montanans. They will not be able to carry the chip of the Civil War on their shoulders for the rest of their lives."

She leaned back in her chair and studied him as Pomp served coffee. "And you," she said. "What will you do?"

"I am not going to Montana," he said.

"No?" she said softly.

He did not look at her for a moment. When he did, he knew what she meant, and yet she was not drawing him on, not using her sex as the bait. "I have made no promises," said Miles.

"Why did you join us?" she asked.

He studied her as she had studied him. "I lost four fine friends back there," he said.

"Is it because of Beck Sterret?"

"Perhaps."

"Revenge is bitter fruit, Miles. Besides, just a moment ago you said the Texans who wanted to stay in Montana could not carry the chip of the Civil Wah on their shoulders for the rest of their lives. Are you not doing the same thing?"

He did not answer. The bawling of the cattle mingled with the howling of the coyotes somehow brought home the solitude of life on the Plains.

Lorena raised her head to listen to the coyotes. "How lonely," she said.

Miles smiled. "One gets used to them. I think I'd miss them if they were not around. I have experienced their loneliness."

"A woman?" she said.

He turned quickly to look at her.

She smiled. "I thought so," she said. "Wheah is she, Miles?"

He shifted in his seat and felt for a cigar, then looked at her.

"Please do," she said. "I have grown accustomed to the weed."

He lighted up and blew a satisfying cloud of smoke.

"You did not answer me, Miles," she said.

He looked at her. "She is in Illinois."

"A long way from Kansas and a longer way from Montana."

He bent his head and looked into the flickering fire. "She died right after the war," he said.

"I'm sorry, Miles."

He waved a hand. "You did not know."

"There have been no others?"

He shrugged. "I thought so a few times. It ended up as ashes."

"You are still a young man, Miles."

"I have not yet found a replacement, Lorena. I am not sure I want one."

She was quiet after that. They sat together, wordlessly, looking into the dying fire, listening to the night sounds, and there was a silent companionship between them. She seemed to know him as no other woman, even Ruth, had known him, and yet he knew there could never be anything between them. It would have been far better had he returned to Dodge City,

41

rather than joining the trail herd with a half-mad desire to take vengeance on Beck Sterret. But he knew there would be a reckoning some day, perhaps when least expected, but it would come, perhaps on the Republican, or the Crazy Woman, perhaps even on the Gallatin, if they ever got that far.

"Is Montana a fair land?" she said at last.

He nodded. "The land is wide and open, with freedom and danger. It is a land for the strong, the ambitious, the far-seeking. The breakers of trails."

She glanced sideways at him, for it seemed as though Jonas, instead of Miles, was speaking. They had much in common, these two strong men, and yet they were quite different in other ways.

Miles leaned back in his chair and looked at the fire, instead of at her, almost as though she wasn't there; as though he saw pictures form in the embers of the fire. "Broad expanses of brown prairie, topped here and there by isolated buttes or a range of tree-fringed hills against the blue sky. There are rough breaks along the fresh, swift-flowing streams. Mountains dark-mantled with pine break sharply from the plain. Deeply etched into the vast expanses of prairie are the valleys of the rivers. The Missouri, the Gallatin, the Yellowstone, and all their tributaries. There are badlands, rugged and forbidding, but still with an eerie beauty of their own, with softly blended hues from the hand of the master painter of them all. Blues, grays, and yellowish-browns. The winters can be bitter cold and the summers scorching hot. It is the wind I think of most of all. Restless, everblowing, carrying the scent of the land to you." His voice died away.

Hooves thudded on the hard ground. Jonas Carlisle swung down heavily, and Pomp came to take the gray away.

Lorena looked at Miles. "There is a touch of the poet in you, Miles."

He laughed. "God forbid!" he said.

Jonas came toward the fire. "God forbid what, Miles?" he said.

Miles could have lied, but to this man he could not. "Mrs. Carlisle said I had a touch of the poet in me," he said.

Jonas nodded. "She may have heard that from me," he said.

Miles looked quickly at him. Jonas had taken off his hat and was wiping his brow. "The beeves are restless tonight. Perhaps they know what is ahead of them. I must admit it makes me restless, too. Miles, do you think I am making a mistake?"

Miles took his eyes and thoughts away from the depths of those brown, searching eyes. "I mean to get through," he

42

said from memory. "There is a great future in Montana. I have land there. A great deal of land in the best cattle country in the world. Story broke the way, and the Sioux have closed it. They cannot stand in the way of our progress. They cannot stand in *my* way, Mister Flint! They have closed the way, but someone must reopen it. *I* am that man! It is my destiny!"

It was very quiet around the dying campfire. Lorena Carlisle looked at her husband. Miles Flint looked into the message of the embers and saw things in there that he did not like. Jonas Carlisle slapped his gauntlets against his thick thigh. "By Godfrey," he said softly. "I've heard an echo of myself there."

Miles stood up. "Those were your words not too long ago, Mister Carlisle."

Jonas nodded. He looked at Miles. "I am a man of action, Miles. You know that. Perhaps you know it too well. I offered you the chance to ride with us to the Gallatin. I can use you. Frankly, I need you. Name your price. You can be invaluable to me. Name your price, man!"

Miles tossed his cigar into the fire. "I will ride with you for a time, but as for my price, that no man knows, and I am not even sure I know it myself. Good night, Mrs. Carlisle. Good night, Jonas." He walked off into the shimmering moonlight and in a moment disappeared in the sharply edged shadows of the willows.

Jonas stood there for a long time looking after Miles. He turned slowly. "A strange man, and yet I feel an affinity for him. Can you explain it, Lorena?"

She stood up. "Get rid of him, Jonas, for your own good."

Jonas looked at her uncomprehendingly. "I don't understand. You're talking strangely, Lorena."

She walked out of the dim circle of dying firelight. "For your own good, Jonas, get rid of him." She walked to the Studebaker where her bed was.

Jonas rubbed his heavy jaw. He looked toward the willows and then toward the Studebaker. "I'll be damned," he said.

From across the moonlit prairie came the soft singing of the night herders.

> "The years creep slowly by, Lorena;
>   The snow is on the grass again;
> The sun's low down the sky, Lorena;
>   The frost gleams where the flowers have been.
> But the heart throbs as warmly now
>   As when the summer days were nigh;
> Oh! the sun can never dip so low
>   Adown affection's cloudless sky."

43

"A hundred months have passed, Lorena,
  Since last I held that hand in mine,
And felt the pulse beat fast, Lorena,
  Though mine beat faster than thine.
A hundred months—'twas flowery May,
  When up the hilly slope we climbed,
To watch the dying of the day
  And hear the distant churchbells chime."

CHAPTER FIVE

North from the Smoky Hill, the Saline, the Solomon, Prairie
Dog Creek, and Sappa Creek to the forks of the Republican
rose the slow trail dust. The herd had long ago gained a per-
sonality, the cattle losing their original wildness that had stayed
with them almost into southern Kansas. It was a mixed herd,
steers and cows, harder to handle than a herd of beeves alone,
because of the difference in the strides of cow and steer, but
a more tractable herd than that of beeves alone, which were
much more susceptible to stampeding. There was something
else that tended to slow a mixed herd; the birth of calves almost every time the herd was bedded down, the drivers finding
the newly born on the bedding grounds in the pale light of
the false dawn. A man could tell at a distance how many calves
had entered the world during the night, so soon to leave it,
by the flat cracking of the six-shooters before the sleepy herd
was formed for the trail. The calves could not keep up with
the herd, and the mothers would try to return to them if
they were left behind. In more settled country the calves
had been given to homesteaders or traded for produce, but now
they were in country where the settlers were few and far between, and there would be no settlers at all in Wyoming, north
of Fort Laramie, for that was Sioux country. Besides, summer
was moving swiftly along and winter would follow autumn,
and the herd was barely keeping up to the schedule planned
for it by Jonas Carlisle, despite the skilled efforts of Beck Sterret and his drivers.

Miles Flint was usually up before the dawn, with a cup or
two of Arbuckle's beneath his belt, keeping an eye out for
stray Indians, although these would be more sneak thieves

44

than hard-hitting raiders, nor would they be in enough strength to arrogantly demand as tribute a "wo-haw" or two. None of the drivers, including Sterret himself, had been this far north in Kansas, and Sterret had come to depend on Miles's information as to the trail and the distances to the next watering place, as well as to good bedding ground for the herd. He never spoke to Miles unless it was absolutely necessary, and Miles in his turn avoided the trail boss. Jonas Carlisle was the mediator between them; he needed both of these tough, efficient men, each without a peer in his particular line.

Despite Miles's dislike of Beck Sterret, he had grown to have a grudging respect for the trail boss. Most of the success of a trail drive depended on the trail boss. Most of them were paid a hundred dollars a month as compared to thirty for the trail hands, but Beck Sterret rated more than that. Jonas had likely promised him a bonus of some sort for handling a trail herd in hostile country. Men like Beck Sterret came high. He had to know each man's capabilities and faults. He had to know more than his tough, independent drivers knew. It was his job to make sure there were enough provisions. He assigned men to their positions and saw that they carried out their duties. He was first up in the darkness before dawn and was the last into his hotroll each night, long after most of the men were asleep. He was responsible for knowing what lay ahead of the herd, the type of trail and the location and quantity of water, and for selecting the sites for the noon rest and the night halt. He had to keep check on the number of cattle in the herd and make sure there were no losses. Further, he had to settle all differences between his men, and amongst the hardbitten Texans of the corrida this meant that Sterret must lead as well as drive, and must be as good, or better, than his men in the use of pistol, fists, or boots. There was little trouble of this sort in the Carlisle corrida. Beck Sterret had carefully selected his men back in Texas. There was no room for the careless, the inefficient, the weak, or the troublemaking sort.

There was another leader for the trail herd. The huge ten-year-old brute named Old Brimstone who was the "lead steer." Old Brimstone knew the trail from Texas to Dodge City, Wichita, and Abilene better than most of the trail drivers. Beck Sterret had worked with Old Brimstone for over five years, and the huge steer had worked the trails with other trail bosses before he had teamed with Beck. It had been Sterret who had talked Jonas Carlisle into buying Old Brimstone. From the time he was a mature beef he had become a leader, taking his place at the head of the herd to point the way north, working with the point men, guiding the herd during the long dusty days, not only by example but from the steady ling-ling-ling of the brass bell Beck Sterret had bought out of his own pocket. And even though Old Brimstone had never been north of the Kansas or the Smoky Hill, all Beck Sterret had to do was point him north each morning. The big steer seemed to have a compass in his head or a knowledge unknown to man, and all day long he'd lead the herd, the tinkling of the bell heard by the front steers of the herd, who'd follow Old Brimstone, with the rest of the cows and beeves strung out far behind.

The herd was on the move with the first pale light of dawn when Old Brimstone's clapper was freed from his bell. The trick was never to let the herd know they were under restraint. Each step of the way had to be taken voluntarily but guided in the direction best suited for the drive. This apparent freedom made the cattle more tractable and less likely to be troublesome. Then, too, the longhorns' endurance and hardiness fitted them for the longer drives. They usually lost little weight and could be handled with little expense. In stampedes they'd hold together better than most cattle, were easier to encircle at a run, and rarely split off when the front was turned. Above all, they could shift for themselves, could go farther with less water, and could endure more suffering than other types of cattle.

The Carlisle herd was well "road broke" by the time they had reached central Kansas, kept well strung out, perhaps fifty or sixty feet across, with the point, swing, flank, and drag riders occasionally riding out to drive back a one-eyed steer or a muley. Beck Sterret didn't follow the custom of letting the older, more experienced riders have the honor and comparatively dust-free positions of point. Sterret had his men change position for each day's drive, rotating around the herd, taking the miserable drag in turn, eating dust, keeping the back corners of the herd from spreading out too far, while the sound of their buckskin poppers rose time and time again from the wreathing dust as the stragglers and weaklings were driven back into the herd.

Beck Sterret set his daily mileage at ten to twelve miles, but there were times when the longhorns covered as much as twenty miles a day to reach water; a dry camp was to be avoided because of the danger of stampedes. The nearest way on a trail, according to the axiom, was the shortest distance between waterholes.

The one task Beck Sterret had relinquished without question was that of scouting ahead for the easiest trail and the shortest distance to the next watering place. Miles Flint had replaced him in this duty. Beck Sterret seemed to hate the thought of being out of eyeshot of the herd. More than once

Miles, on his way to or from his duties, had seen Beck riding at the head of the herd, between the point riders, sometimes with his left hand resting on the wicked-looking tip of Old Brimstone's right horn, while the steer walked in rhythm with Beck's horse. The lead steer and the trail boss seemed to have something in common; none of the trail drivers or anyone else with the corrida seemed to have Beck Sterret's friendship or confidence. They seemed to suit each other, Miles thought more than once, for both of them were leaders, and like the captain of a ship or the leader of an army they must keep to themselves to avoid familiarity with their subordinates.

There was another thought that ate at Miles Flint's mind, and it had a direct correlation to the fact that Beck Sterret had let Miles take over his duties of riding ahead of the herd. *If Beck Sterret had been riding ahead, as he should have been, his herd would never have stampeded the buffalo herd that had wiped out Miles's skinning camp on the fork of the Smoky Hill. If Beck Sterret was waiting until the herd reached the Gallatin to settle any smoldering differences, he should surely know by now that Miles Flint too had a score to settle in the valley of Gallatin . . . if he stayed with the herd that far.*

The Platte was the next major goal of the trail herd, and from there the trail would trend northwesterly, following the Oregon Trail as far as Ogallala, thence branching off, following the North Platte to Fort Laramie. Miles had first thought of leaving the herd at the Republican, then had changed it to the North Platte, and now thought increasingly of Fort Laramie. It might be fitting to leave the trail herd there, where he had joined Nelson Story for his epic trail-breaking drive to Montana. Yet something held Miles Flint with the herd, although he constantly tried to drive the thought from his mind. It was Lorena Carlisle, and yet nothing had passed between them to hold them together other than the deep-seated feeling Miles had recognized within himself. He did not really know how she felt about him, but he felt her presence, particularly during the nights when he lay on his bed looking up at the stars, knowing she was sleeping within a few minutes' walk of him, or perhaps staring up at the white tilt of the Studebaker over her, sleepless as Miles was sleepless. He wanted to leave the trail herd because of her, and yet he had to stay because of her, and now he knew the meaning of a curse upon one's self.

The long, sun-soaked days passed as the herd moved toward the Platte. Now and then a solitary Indian would be seen sitting his paint pony, watching the dust-shrouded herd, thinking he was well out of rifle range of the strange white men who drove the stinking spotted buffalo through country that had known little but the hoofprints of buffalo and horses. None of these solitary Indians knew that the Texans carried the fast-loading, long-range, accurate Remingtons, or that the white scout who rode far ahead of the herd carried a rifle that could kill easily at half a mile. This was not truly hostile Indian country as yet, but thievery was rampant. Already the herds of buffalo were diminishing, and the fringe tribes of the plains were trying to accustom themselves to the taste of the stinking spotted buffalo. Nor were they averse to snapping up a lone rider, a stray horse, or perhaps a wagon that had fallen too far behind the rest of the wagons and out of protection of the rifles of the trail drivers.

The herd camped and bedded on the North Platte, just north of Big Springs, near the confluence of the North Platte with Blue Creek, for the weeding out of the herd weaklings, the reshoing of the horses and mules, and adding some trail meat to the frames of the cattle. Jonas Carlisle took three wagons and rode into Ogallala for supplies to feed his drivers as far as Fort Laramie.

Times had changed along the North Platte even in the few years that had passed since Miles had last seen it before his ride with Nelson Story to Montana. In those days there had been emigrant trains along the valley of the North Platte, following the Oregon Trail. Now the Union Pacific had extended from Kearny all the way to Cheyenne. There had been warlike groups of Indians along the North Platte, but now there were a few scattered groups—roached-hair Pawnees and slim, slovenly Arikaras, many of them dressed like white men, with a few Poncas and Otoes and perhaps a handful of Arapahoes, still untamed. They came to beg, to steal, and to get drunk and challenge all comers to wild horse races. Many of them were outcasts from their tribes, with little or none of the fierce pride and independence of the warriors who rode with Red Cloud. But there were those who passed on the word about the huge trail herd feeding along the North Platte, not being loaded aboard the cattle cars to be taken east as other herds had been, and the talk was that the herd would move west, along the North Platte, and even farther, but none of the informants were sure just where the herd was bound, nor would any of the people with the herd say where it was bound.

One evening, as Miles Flint rode toward the bedded herd, the campfire smoke hung low over the camp, mingling with a faint mist that arose from the bottoms and partly concealing about half of the great herd. Farther upstream was the wagon camp, upwind of the herd to avoid the smell and heat of the cattle. The blinking red eyes of the campfires were like rubies cast on dark velvet, and some of the wagon tilts were showing faintly yellow from the light of the lanterns that hung within them. One of them would be the Studebaker occupied by Lorena Carlisle, for Jonas Carlisle was seldom in it, sleeping many times with the men or tumbling exhausted into bed only late at night. She was so young and beautiful. The thought was in Miles's mind as he passed the herd, hearing the soft singing of the night herders riding along the flanks of the herd. The herd was quiet. The weather had been exceptionally fine, but there would be thunder and lightning storms and lashing rains farther west and north as the summer died and the fall came on. Now and then a steer or cow would arise, graze a little, then bed down again.

Miles swung down near the chuckwagon, avoiding the huddled forms of the sleeping drivers. He ground-reined the tired bay. He had passed the day before and the night farther along the North Platte, asking questions, talking to anyone who had information about the Bozeman Trail and the activities of the Sioux. A cavalry platoon had been escorting a small supply train from the railroad toward Fort Laramie, but the only information their commander could give Miles was that Regulars were being moved west to take over garrison duty and patrol duty from some of the militia and volunteer outfits that had held those duties during the war and for some time after it. Further, many of the Regulars were recruits, new to the frontier, and their officers, many of whom were war veterans, were inexperienced in fighting Indians. In short, the Army west of Kansas and Nebraska was small in numbers, poorly equipped, and lacking in Indian-fighting experience. The Bozeman Trail was still closed by the Sioux, although they had been quiet all that summer, but then there had been no travelers on the Bozeman. Further, although the Army might advise travelers to stay away from the Bozeman, they had no authority to prevent them from leaving Fort Laramie, nor did they have the strength to turn back all travelers. There was one other thing. Neither did they have the strength to challenge Red Cloud in his own country.

Miles walked to the banked fire and withdrew the smoke-blackened coffeepot. He filled a cup and lighted a cigar leaning against the side of the chuckwagon. Ernie Masland was fast asleep in the front of the wagon, now that all the hotrolls usually loaded in the chuckwagon were being used. Besides, Ernie was usually up even before Beck Sterret. Miles eyed the sleeping drivers. Nothing short of a cannon shot or the strident voice of Beck Sterret would rouse them from their well-earned rest.

Something moved in the darkness beyond the wagon. Miles

49

lowered the cup from his lips. He narrowed his eyes as a large form took shape, and then he grinned. It was Old Brimstone. The lead steer considered himself an individual apart from the masses. He often walked right into the camp and made himself known to the cocinero for a handout of bread, meat, dried apples, or anything else he could cadge. Miles felt about the back of the wagon and found a hard loaf of bread. He walked to the steer and held it out to him. The end of the steer's picket line trailed off into the darkness beyond the wagon. It was likely he had pulled the pin free from the ground or away from the scrub tree to which it had been tied, but then he wouldn't wander far from his bedding place except perhaps to graze with the remuda, as he accepted them as workers, as he was, rather than his inferiors, the cattle of the herd.

Miles got the bay and led him toward the place where he would make his own bed. Old Brimstone wandered after him, and Miles grinned in the darkness. The lead steer was at least more friendly than his boss, Beck Sterret, and was quite a pet with the trail drivers, except when Sterret was around and then he was Sterret's personal pet.

Miles passed beyond the chuckwagon and the group of sleeping drivers, then through a motte of willows and cottonwoods. He could see the faint lightness of the Studebaker wagon tilts in the darkness. He picketed the bay near the creek and unsaddled him. He dropped the saddle near his bedroll and glanced toward the Studebakers. This was one night he was glad that there was no light on in Lorena Carlisle's wagon, or that she was not seated alone beside the fire, while Jonas was with the herd or talking with Beck Sterret.

Old Brimstone had stopped twenty feet from Miles. He raised his head into the wind, blowing fresher from upstream past the Studebakers. He was poised almost like a pointer hound. Miles looked at him curiously. A low, almost imperceptible sound came from the big steer. Miles looked toward the wagons. There wasn't a sign of life there. Pomp was probably fast asleep, but Jonas usually had a man assigned as guard near the wagons. Miles dropped his cigar and rubbed it out on the ground. Old Brimstone lowered his head and swung it from side to side. Something was bothering him.

Miles walked toward the wagons. He could just make out the lighter coloring of the faded tilts. The fire was long out, probably thick with ashes. The faint odor of it came to Miles on the wind. He looked back at the steer. Something came back to him, something Ernie Masland had told him one evening. Old Brimstone had once been separated in a storm from a trail herd and had been cut off by hungry Kiowas; when returned to the herd, there was blood on his horntips and an arrow stuck in his flank. From then on, Ernie had said, Old Brimstone had recognized the smell of Indians.

Miles wet his lips and padded toward the wagons. The guard should be close to the wagons, and Miles didn't want a Remington slug in his guts, at least before breakfast. He whistled softly. There was no reply. He shoved back his hat and peered closely at the wagons. If Old Brimstone had a nose for Indians, Miles Flint had one for unseen danger. It had kept him alive through four years of war and while scouting for the Army and later hunting buffalo.

He stopped at the front of the first wagon. It was used to carry the camping gear and other stores. He placed his hand on the butt of his Remington. The wind shifted, whirling the top layer of ashes from the fire, revealing faint red eyes in the thick embers. Then it came to him, the feeling of danger, stronger than ever, and with it a faintly rancid smell as of sour grease. He whirled, freeing the Remington, and a dark form struck at him. Something drove into his right bicep and the shock of it made him drop the Remington. He bent low, driving a shoulder into the gut of his attacker, lifting him on his shoulders and throwing his body backward so that the man fell heavily. Miles smashed a foot down on the man's knife wrist, but the man did not move.

Another dark form rounded the wagon. A woman screamed. It was Lorena. Miles saw her white form against the darkness of the man who held her. He closed in, fending off another knife, hurling Lorena to one side to get her out of the way. He gripped the knife wrist of the man and twisted hard, catching the knife as it fell. As he arose he drove the knife in deep, just below the ribs, twisting the blade and ripping sideways in a figure-seven stroke. He kicked the man in the belly, driving him back so that he fell half across the fire.

Miles staggered sideways, the sweat streaming down his face and the hot blood running down his arm. It was only then that he saw her nakedness. He gripped his arm and swayed a little until he could hold his balance. Somewhere in the darkness a man yelled. Miles rounded the back of the wagon.

The tall form stood in front of Miles and the hammer of the pistol double-clicked back. "Yuh Yankee sonofabitch," said the voice of Beck Sterret. "What did yuh do to thet woman?"

Miles was closer to death now than he had been fighting the two prowlers. "Go look, you Texas bastard," he grated through pain-clenched teeth.

"Mis' Carlisle?" called out Sterret.

51

"Yes, Beckwith," she said from the darkness of the wagon. "It wasn't Mister Flint. He saved me."

Suddenly the fire flared up and the odor of burning cloth and flesh came to them. Beck Sterret rounded the back of the wagon with softly chiming spurs. The flickering firelight showed the first man Miles had fought lying with his neck twisted at an unnatural angle, his sightless eyes reflecting the firelight. The other man lay face down in the revived fire, supplying the fuel for it. Beck Sterret hooked a boot toe under him and rolled him free of the fire. The smoke rose from the burning clothing and revealed the great killing wound Miles had made in the man's gut.

Boots pounded on the hard ground. Ernie Masland rounded the first wagon, rifle in hand. "That you, Miles?" he called.

"Yes, Ernie," said Miles. "I'm cut bad."

"Who were they?" said Chip Macklin, one of the wagon drivers, as he came into the pool of firelight.

"They might be Rees," said Miles. "They're Indians, all right. Maybe breeds. Sneak thieves. Killers if they can get away with it."

Beck Sterret nodded. "Are yuh all right, Mis' Carlisle?" he said.

"Yes, Beck. Thanks to Miles Flint."

Sterret made no recognition of Miles. "Who was supposed to be on guard heah, Chip?" he said.

"Frank Jeffers," said Chip.

Beck nodded again. "Tell him to pack up and git out. Tonight! Now! I don't want to catch sight of him evah again."

Chip vanished into the darkness.

Miles bent down and picked up the wadded night dress that had been ripped from Lorena's body. He handed it to her, then walked with Ernie toward the chuckwagon. He looked back at Beck Sterret. "You'd better get a spade detail, Sterret," he said. "Those boys might have friends around here. Bury 'em and hide any traces of it."

"I know my business," said the trail boss.

"Is that right?" said Miles. His meaning was clear enough. Those wagons should have never been left unguarded. He walked on toward the chuckwagon, never looking back, but he could almost feel those cold gray eyes boring into his back. Beck Sterret allowed no man in his corrida to make a mistake, but Beck Sterret had made one himself that night.

Ernie doused the wound with whiskey and swabbed it, leaving the rest of the whiskey for internal application by Miles. As he finished binding the deep wound, hoofbeats sounded in the darkness and drummed on the hard ground until they faded away. Ernie looked up. "That'll be Frank Jeffers," he said.

"Beck Sterret allows no mistakes," said Chip Macklin.

Miles lowered the whiskey bottle and handed it to Ernie. "Who takes Beck Sterret to account for his mistakes? God?" he said dryly. He saw the look on Chip's face. Miles turned. The trail boss stood by the fire looking at Miles, and this time Miles caught the full impact of those eyes and he knew that never on God's green earth would he and this man ever be anything but enemies.

CHAPTER SIX

The grass along the North Platte was good, and the longhorns put on some tallow despite the fact that they were being driven harder, doing better than twenty miles a day for the most part, for the water was always there for the noon rest and the night camp. But the summer was beginning to fade. Now and then a spit of rain fell, and the nights grew cooler. In the mornings dew spangled the grass, the wagon covers, and the bedrolls with crystal droplets. The days became smoky with haze, but the nights were bright and clear and the moon was large and luminous.

Past Rush Creek and Pumpkin Creek toward Scotts Bluff they trailed, passing the slowly moving emigrant trains and being passed in turn by the Abbott-Downing "swiftwagons" of the stagecoach lines, with wondering drivers and passengers eyeing the great herd of dusty cattle and the expressionless sunbrowned, longhaired men who drove them ever westward. There was no need for anyone who learned about their ultimate destination to comment too much about such folly, but it went something as follows. "They won't get to the Gallatin. They won't even get past the Powder. They'll likely lose that hull durned herd and their own scalps as well. Ain't nobody more loco than a Texican. This proves it. Jonas Carlisle is supplyin' beef on the hoof to the Sioux and the Cheyennes for the comin' winter. He's leavin' that woman at Fort Laramie, ain't he? *He ain't?* There'll be a half-breed in a Sioux lodge 'bout this time next year." So on and so on, and it never stopped, past Scotts Bluff and into Wyoming on the well-worn trail, the great highway of emigrant travel to the Far West.

They crossed the Laramie River at the end of August to graze the herd northwest of the fort, making camp on a creek that flowed into the Laramie five miles from the fort. It was a time for some rest and to let the longhorns gain a little more tallow for the long trail north to the Gallatin. It was time too for the trail drivers to sport in the disreputable "hog ranches" situated just off the fort reservation. These were stocked with the worst rotgut booze and worked by aging, bedraggled and usually diseased painted ladies and calico cats, perhaps their last port of call before they were through with their trade, for they could not work anywhere else because of the competition except near some lonely Army post far away from any sort of town.

Colonel Denton Long paced back and forth in his headquarters office, with a government map of the country north of Fort Laramie forming a background for the words he was speaking to the three men who sat beyond his desk. Miles Flint was studying the map, recalling geographical features from the symbols on the flat paper. Straight up the center of the map ran a red line, the Bozeman Trail, with red crosses indicating the sites of the forts built after the war, occupied for a short time, then abandoned by the Army and burned by the Sioux.

"Two hundred and fifty miles of unguarded territory," said the colonel. "Not a post, a house, a road other than the Bozeman; not a soldier between here and Montana! Even beyond the Wyoming line you won't be safe from the Sioux—not that you'd ever get there."

"Nelson Story made it," said Carlisle stubbornly.

Jonas blew a smoke ring from his cigar. "Nelson Story made it without the help of the Army, Colonel," he said. "No offense to the Army, of course."

"The Army had all it could do in those days, as it does even now, to defend itself," said Long.

"Miles here was with Story," said Carlisle.

Miles smiled wryly. "I was younger then," he said. "Fortune favors the brave, or so they say."

Long sat down and fiddled with a letter opener fashioned like a miniature saber. "Do you intend to ride with Mister Carlisle, Miles?" he said.

Carlisle smiled. Sterret rubbed his lean jaw and felt for the makings.

Miles looked at the map. How well he knew that trail. Every mile and every topographical feature was etched on his memory. From Fort Fetterman on the Platte north to Willow Creek and Sand Creek, Antelope Creek and Pumpkin Buttes east of the Dry Fork of the Powder, past old Fort Reno and the Crazy Woman Battlefield of 1866, to the crossing of the Crazy Woman.

"Miles?" said the officer.

Miles started a little. It was as though he was bringing his mind back from those dangerous, lonely miles of Wyoming.

"Of course he is," said Jonas Carlisle. "Miles has placed his destiny with mine, Colonel Long."

"I didn't think Miles was that big a fool," said Long. "I've known him since the war. I was surprised when he went with Nelson Story. I was sure he had learned his lesson then. How about it, Miles?"

Miles looked away from the map. "Yes," he said quickly. "I did learn my lesson. Perhaps Mister Carlisle can get through. I hope he can."

Carlisle stared incredulously at Miles. "But you *are* riding with us!"

Miles shook his head. "I never agreed to ride to the Gallatin," he said.

Carlisle slowly took the cigar from his mouth. "But I have been depending on you."

"What did you expect from *him?*" said Beck Sterret.

Miles stood up. "I agreed to ride north with you, first as far as the Republican and then as far as the North Platte. Then I decided to stay with you as far as Fort Laramie. This I have done. I made no promises beyond riding with you to Fort Laramie."

Carlisle relighted his cigar. He looked up at Miles and fanned out the match. "Are you holding me up, Miles?"

"I wouldn't put it past him," growled Sterret.

Miles narrowed his eyes. "I don't follow you, Jonas," he said quietly.

"Name your price," said the trail driver. "A part of the herd? A piece of my land in Montana? A sum of money? Name it, Miles."

Miles shook his head. "You couldn't pay me with the whole herd, Jonas. It isn't that."

"Then dammit, what is it?"

It was then that Beck Sterret's cold gray eyes flicked up at Miles, and Miles knew that the Texan knew why Miles would go no further. By God, he knew!

Miles walked to the door. "I am returning to Kansas," he said. "Buffalo running is my trade. I've been away from it long enough as it is."

"There's a job here for you, Miles," said Colonel Long quickly. "Chief of Scouts."

Miles shook his head.

"Think about it, Miles," said the officer.

Miles closed the door behind him and lighted a cigar. He stood on the porch for a few minutes, looking across the wide, dark parade ground. Yellow rectangles of light showed from the windows of the post buildings. The halyards rattled insistently against the tall flagpole. It would be a rough fall and an early winter from the feeling in the night air. He looked to his left, to the north, into the star-spangled darkness of the prairie night. Beck Sterret had sensed or had figured out why Miles would not accompany the trail herd any further than Fort Laramie. He wanted to go, and could not go, for the very same reason. It was simple enough. It could be answered in two lovely words. *Lorena Carlisle.*

The feeling had come upon him with increasing intensity each day and each week of the long trail north to the Platte River country, particularly since that bloody night beside Blue Creek when he had killed the two Indians, full-bloods or breeds, who had attacked him after their failure to rape or abduct Lorena. His memories of that night were strong because of the wound he had suffered, but there was more than that. Since seeing her in her nakedness he had not been able to drive the thought from his mind. Perhaps he loved her, he really didn't know, although the emotion he felt for her was close enough to be labeled love. But night after night he would lie awake, staring up into the darkness, seeing her as he had seen her in that vivid moment, and he could *not* drive the picture of her from his mind.

He could not let her ride up that dangerous trail to the north, for the odds against the trail herd getting through were very high. He had hoped Carlisle would change his mind and take the western trail, thence through the mountain passes north to Montana, but it was getting late in the season, with the promise of an early winter. There was one other hope. Perhaps Jonas could be persuaded to leave his wife at Fort Laramie until he could send for her in the spring via the western route. But it was not up to Miles Flint to try to persuade Jonas Carlisle, inasmuch as Miles himself was not going to Montana with the trail herd. Not with Beck Sterret already suspecting, if he did not already know, how Miles felt about Lorena.

The truth was that he could not trust himself with her; he thought too much of her and of Jonas as well. It was better this way, and yet . . .

Tattoo blew softly across the post and echoed faintly from the dark hills. Miles could hear the voices of the three men in the colonel's office and then the popping of a cork, followed by the clinking of glass. It looked like a long session, for Jonas Carlisle was a stubborn man; so, too, was Denton Long.

Miles breathed the clear night air. A faint longing came to him for the brass and the blue, the regularity of garrison life, spiced by the occasional Indian fighting and the lonely, dangerous scouting. He shook his head. He had been on his own too long; too long a buffalo runner. Miles walked to the end of the long porch and stepped down upon the gravel path that led past the colonel's quarters. Beyond the quarters was a smaller building, once used by the second-in-command of the post but no longer occupied. Miles walked toward the building. Colonel Long had found him a room at Old Bedlam, the junior officers' quarters, which was more than half empty of occupants.

He paused in front of the empty building and relighted the cigar, the flare of the match in the night wind lighting his lean face. He fanned out the match and drew in a deep breath of the satisfying smoke. There was a bottle in his war sack in his quarters.

He raised his head suddenly. An alertness honed by years of warfare, danger, and hunting had warned him. He took the cigar from his mouth and looked at the empty building. Faintly, ever so faintly, the odor of lilac scent came to him. He shook his head. There was no one there. A cold feeling came over him. Ruth had worn such scent. There were many ghosts at Fort Laramie and beyond, but it wasn't likely the ghost of Ruth Flint would be there. He took one step and paused. He turned and looked at the darkened porch of the quarters. There *was* someone there!

"Miles?" she said out of the darkness.

"Ruth?" he blurted out.

The wind shifted. A door slammed from somewhere in the barracks across the dark parade ground. The flagpole halyards beat the pole in a sudden frenzy. The odor of the lilac scent came strongly to Miles.

She came to the edge of the porch and looked down at him. "Ruth?" she said softly. "Where you expecting a *Ruth*, Miles?"

He pulled off his hat and took the cigar from his mouth. His face flushed in the darkness. "Mrs. Carlisle," he said.

"Lorena, Miles."

"I did not know you were here."

"Colonel Long was kind enough to allow my husband to use these quarters."

"I thought you were camped with the trail herd."

"It's very lonely out theah, Miles. Some of the boys were

riding into the fort and escorted me heah. Jonas doesn't know I am heah. Is he still in conference?"

Miles nodded. "Very much so."

"Come heah, Miles."

He walked toward her and stood at the foot of the steps.

"Is the colonel going to allow Jonas to take the Bozeman Trail?"

Miles shrugged. "He can hardly stop him. He *can* advise him not to."

"And you are against it?"

"Yes."

"And yet you are going, too. Why, Miles?"

He looked up into that shadowy, lovely face, and he could not speak.

"Miles?" she said. "What's wrong?"

"I'm not going to the Gallatin with the trail herd," he said.

It was her turn to be speechless. She stared uncomprehendingly at him and shook her head a little. "I don't understand," she said uncertainly.

"I made no promises. No deals," he said.

"But it was understood. Jonas said . . ." Her voice trailed off.

He knew now what he had wondered about before. There had always been a kind of understanding between them so that neither really had to speak to let his or her thoughts be known. He thanked God he had been able to keep away from her so much on the trail along the Platte to Fort Laramie. If she had been able to read some of his thoughts then . . .

"Jonas planned to repay you for your troubles," she said.

"It isn't that, Lorena. You *know* it isn't that."

She nodded and looked away, toward the north, toward the unseen Bozeman, as he had done a few minutes before she had spoken his name from the clinging darkness of the porch. She knew well enough that payment was the furthest thing from his mind. What payment would he want? She thought uncertainly that she might know what that could be, then thrust it quickly from her mind, for she herself had thought much, far too much about this lean hunter of buffaloes and swift killer of men.

"You must not go with them," said Miles desperately.

She looked down at him. "My place is with my husband," she said softly.

"There is a madness in him," said Miles. "Nelson Story had it; at times I have had it myself. But it *is* madness, Lorena. You can't go with him."

She tilted her lovely head to one side. "What is it you want me to do, Miles?"

"You can stay here until the spring and then travel to Montana via the west, then through the passes. He can send for you then, or you can travel with one of the strong parties that will travel west when the trails dry out."

"But you do not believe he will evah send for me. You believe he will die on the Bozeman."

Softly across the post came the sweet, melancholy sound of taps, floating over the parade ground, bringing with it many memories to the fighting men who had heard it at other. less peaceful times. It echoed softly, almost imperceptibly from the hills. Lights flicked out one after the other, and the darkness, purring softly with the voice of the dry night wind, crept closer and ever closer to the man and woman who faced each other.

"Miles?" she said.

He nodded. "I can't bear to see you go," he said, "and I can't bear to go with you."

"And if I stay heah, what will you do? Will you leave, Miles? Will you forget about me? Will you *try* to forget about me?"

"That is unfair," he said quickly.

She reached out a hand, and the tips of her cool fingers touched his face. "Yes," she said wisely and softly. "I know and you know, Miles. We can't drive it from our minds."

He stepped up to her. She backed away a little but then stopped and came close to him, into his arms, her face tilted up to his. He bent to kiss her, and she turned her soft, full lips away. Her fragrance and softness made him a little savage. He cupped her chin in his left hand, turning her face to meet his lips. Her body was tense for a moment, then she pressed close to him and her lips sought his as eagerly, perhaps more eagerly than his had sought hers, and their bodies were as closely molded together in the darkness as could be possible, with one exception.

She bent back her head. "Come with us, Miles," she said fiercely. *"Come with me."*

"Stay here," he replied. "Stay here with me."

A door rattled somewhere in the darkness. Porch boards creaked. Lorena stepped back from Miles. "Oh God," she said. "I didn't mean to. I still love my husband, Miles!"

He placed a big hand alongside her face and looked into her eyes. Dark as it was, he seemed to be able to see deeply into them. "Yes," he said softly, and he knew she didn't mean it at all.

Spurs chimed softly on the gravel.

Miles touched her lips with his, then walked softly to the end of the porch. He heard the door close as she entered the building. Miles stepped around the corner feeling as guilty

59

as a thief, which perhaps he was in a sense. A thief of love belonging to another man, a man he admired, respected, and called friend.

Miles faded back into the darkness as the spurs chimed again. The chiming stopped. Miles stepped behind an outthrust part of the frame building. The chiming started again, so soft as to be almost indistinct. Miles pressed back against the wall behind him.

There was a quick spurt of yellow, flickering light beyond the building that showed the lean, hard face of Beck Sterret as he cupped the flame about the tip of a cigarette. He fanned out the match. Alternately the glowing and dying away of the tip of the cigarette lighted his face and then let it fade into the darkness beneath the low-pulled hatbrim. Beck Sterret seemed to be looking directly at Miles. Beck turned and looked across the dark parade ground, and as he did so the window alongside Miles glowed with the light of a lamp. Miles cursed under his breath, then slipped along the wall and rounded the corner just as Sterret turned again. Miles was around the corner perhaps a fraction of a second ahead of Beck's piercing gaze —or perhaps a fraction of a second too late.

Still, Beck Sterret would need the eyes of a cat to identify any shadowy figure he might have seen. At that, Miles wouldn't put it past the Texan to be able to see in the dark.

Miles walked toward the dim shape of the icehouse, to keep the commanding officer's quarters between him and Beck Sterret. He walked along the edge of the bluff that skirted the old channel of the Laramie River. He could see the dim, pewter-colored water of the river just beyond the old channel. He looked back over his shoulder. There was no sign of Beck Sterret or anyone else.

He was just passing the provost marshal's office when a thought struck him like the blow of a Sioux pipe-axe. He turned on his heel and looked toward the commanding officer's quarters. The lights were still on in Long's office, and there was a lone light in the quarters that had been loaned to Carlisle. That would be Lorena. No wonder Beck Sterret had been suspicious! Miles had dropped his freshlly lit cigar on the gravel directly in front of the porch steps of the quarters occupied by Jonas and Lorena. Miles shoved back his hat. He had left Long's office only a few minutes before Beck. Trust Beck Sterret to have heard Lorena's door close and, perhaps, their low voices. He could hardly have missed seeing or smelling that cigar. What if he had seen a shadowy figure moving about behind the building? He knew who was in that building alone, and he had certainly seen that light go on in the otherwise unlighted quarters.

Miles hadn't looked for a meeting with Lorena. Had she looked for a meeting with him? *Had she been waiting for him?* There was guilt within him, more for his thoughts than for any of his actions. He had wanted to avoid her because he had realized that seeing her would lead to no good for both of them. Neither of them could willingly deceive Jonas.

He stepped up on the porch of Old Bedlam and looked toward Lorena's quarters. Even as he did so the light winked out. She was likely in bed, thinking of him, and the thought of it was almost too much for him to bear. He opened the door and walked quietly down the hall to his room. There was only one other officer quartered on the first floor that night, and he was on guard duty. There were a number of junior officers quartered on the second floor, but most of them were either on patrol or escort details, shorthanded as the post was of officers.

Miles opened the door, and the light from within struck his tense face. He had not left the lamp on. The lampshade had been tilted up toward the door, casting a pool of light on the tabletop and the floor around it as well as on the doorway, but keeping the rest of the room in darkness.

"I've been waitin' for yuh, Flint," said Beck Sterret from the darkness beyond the lamp.

There was no chance for Miles to draw or run. He raised his head. "What's the game, Sterret?" he said evenly.

Spurs chimed. Miles still could not see the man.

"I'm ridin' back to the herd tonight," said the trail boss.

"Can't bear to stay away from those longhorns?" said Miles.

"Very funny," said the Texan. "But then yuh got a great sense of humor, for a Yankee."

"Gracias," said Miles.

"Por nada," said Beck.

The lamplight was full on Miles's face. What could Beck Sterret see in it? Why was he stalling?

A match snapped in the darkness, and the flare of it revealed Beck's face as he lighted a quirly. Miles could have drawn and shot fast enough to kill the Texan before he could draw, fast as he was reputed to be.

The cigarette glowed as Sterret drew in the smoke. His cold gray eyes studied Miles. "Yuh shouldn't ought to have let Jonas down," he said.

"That was between him and me, Sterret."

The Texan nodded. "I agree. But thet herd is goin' to Montana come hell or high watah, Flint! We can't stand the sight of each othah, but I got to admit we need yuh. God knows I wish it was othawise, but it ain't."

"Gracias," said Miles dryly.

61

Sterret took the cigarette from his mouth and studied the tip of it. "Thet herd means a lot to me, Flint."

"And nothing else does."

The head snapped up. "Damn yuh! Stop boring into me, Flint! Yuh know so damned much! Mebbe yuh don't know what Jonas Carlisle means to me! He's treated me fair and square and give me a future to look forward to outside of bein' a trail boss. Yuh know what thet means to a man like me? No kin to speak of. No home to go back to. Not a centavo put aside. I'm gettin' along. I don't aim to trail boss all my life, not thet I couldn't make most of 'em look like second raters for yeahs to come!"

"I'll buy that," said Miles. Give the devil his due, he thought. "How about a drink?"

"No," said Sterret.

"Mind if I have one?" Miles wanted to get out of that revealing pool of light.

"Go ahead," said the Texan.

Miles walked to his bag and dug out a bottle.

"Yuh won't reconsider?" said Sterret.

God how it must have eaten into his Texas pride to have to ask a Yankee, and Miles Flint of all Yankees, for help. "No," said Miles.

Sterret paused. Miles glanced at him. The cigarette lighted his face. Miles looked down at his drink.

"Then theah's Mis' Carlisle to consider," said Beck.

Miles left hand closed about the full shot glass. Here it comes! Maybe he could throw the liquor into Sterret's face and close with him before he could draw. "What about Mrs. Carlisle?" said Miles quietly.

"She ain't goin' to stay heah," said Beck.

"So?" said Miles. He turned to look at Sterret.

The Texan seemed at a loss for words. "She means a lot to me, to all of us, mebbe even to you, Flint." There was no obvious guile in his words. "Yuh saw what happened back theah on the Platte. If it hadn't been for yuh, Flint, she'da been raped or killed. Mebbe worse. Mebbe drug off to a filthy Indian camp somewheahs. Yuh follow me?"

"So far," said Miles politely.

Sterret moved, and the spurs chimed. He came closer to Miles. Miles tensed for swift and deadly action. "Jonas ain't right in lettin' her go along, but he will if she insists, and she *does* insist. We might get through and we might not, but I don't aim to see anything happen to her. Understand?"

Miles nodded. He sipped at the rye.

Sterret came closer. "It ain't for me I'm askin' yuh to come along, but for Jonas and his wife. He said once thet he needed yuh. Thet yuh know the Bozeman Trail and the ways of the Sioux. With thet Sharps of yourn yuh could hold off fifty Sioux and never raise a sweat. He said he needed yuh. We need every advantage we can get, Flint."

For a long, long moment Miles stood there. "Indians," he said. "All they ever do is beg for sugar, tobacco, whiskey, and a wo-haw or two. A taste of powdersmoke will drive them off like gnats before a smudge fire. Those were your words, Sterret, the first time I met you. Maybe you've changed your mind."

"Don't be cute, Flint."

Miles turned. "If you and Carlisle are fools enough to go up the Bozeman, you'll have to take the guilt of anything that happens to Mrs. Carlisle. For me, I want no part of it."

"Is thet final?"

"It is."

Sterret nodded. He walked to the door, gripped the handle, then turned so that the light from under the uptilted lampshade revealed his lean face and glacial eyes. "I mighta knowed," he said. "I left yuh alone because of Jonas. I kept the boys away from yuh because of Jonas. I stood for yore lip because of Jonas. But that's all ovah now, Flint."

"So?" said Miles.

A faint smile drifted across the lean face, but there was no trace of it in the set eyes of the Texan. "Maybe it's best this way," he said softly. "If we evah reached the Gallatin, one of us woulda had to kill yuh, Flint. It's in the cards."

Miles bent his head. *"Gracias,"* he said.

"Por nada," said Sterret politely. He opened the door. "One more thing: Stay away from the Gallatin valley, Flint. Don't evah show yore face up theah. *Evah . . ."*

Miles poured another drink. The door closed behind the Texan. Miles downed the liquor. He heard the spurs chime down the hall and then fade away. A few moments later he heard the soft tattoo of hooves on the hard ground, and then they too faded away.

Miles sat down on the bed and slowly wiped the icy sweat from his face. He still didn't know whether or not Beck Sterret suspected or knew Miles had been with Lorena. Maybe he had concealed it because he had wanted Miles to rejoin the trail herd. Maybe, just maybe . . .

CHAPTER SEVEN

The breed rode out of the Laramie River bottoms below Fort Laramie, leaving the filthy skin lodges of the Indians who hung about the fort looking for handouts, doing occasional scouting of dubious value, and selling the services of their women to the drunken troopers. It was the night before Jonas Carlisle's trail herd was to leave for the Bozeman Trail.

The breed's given name was François Gaspard Bertillot. He himself hardly remembered that name. White men, breeds, and full-bloods who knew him simply called him Guts. He had no friends and no relatives. His mother had been a dull-witted girl of the Sans Arcs, while his father, whom he had never known, had been half white, half Negro, and all bad.

Guts rode toward the headwaters of Rawhide Creek with his news. It was how he lived. He picked up information and sold it, to white man or to red—it mattered not as long as he was given food or anything he required. In more civilized areas he would be called "informer." Here his name served the same as such a title. "Ask Guts," one would say if he was asked anything he did not know about the country, the Indians, or the soldiers. Somehow Guts would know, or he would find out. It was how he lived, for all men's hands were against him, although their ears were not, as they sought and bought his information. He lived as a pariah and liked it. That way he was safe, for although he had no friends and no relatives, he had no true enemies either, and he could do what no hostile Indian or white man could do—ride with impunity in either country and go unchallenged.

The trail herd groaned its way along the North Platte road in the cold light of a misty dawn the morning after Guts had gone north to the Rawhide. They would be heading for Fort Fetterman, west of La Prele Creek. From there they would go northwesterly to the Bozeman Trail and the country of the Sioux.

Miles Flint had left Fort Laramie the morning after his talk with Beck Sterret. He had not seen Jonas and Lorena leave the fort and ride out to the trail camp. Miles had not been there, but part of him had gone along with them, and he knew it would never come back to him. A man cannot lose his heart too many times, perhaps only once. He knew he had loved his wife, but the mists of time had closed in, and he was still a young man. His heart had gone with Lorena Carlisle. It would be better if he did not follow it. Miles stayed with an old friend of his, Pete Lingle, who had served with him as a scout at Fort Laramie. Pete had taken over the site of old Fort Bernard, across the Platte from Fort Laramie some miles downstream. Good talk and good liquor, along with the fine cooking of Lingle's Ute squaw, had made the days drift past for Miles, on the long road in time he would have to cover before the face of Lorena faded from his memory.

A faint, misty rain was falling in the valley of the Platte when Miles rode toward the yellow lights of the fort. It was dusk, but it seemed later to Miles. Some of the fumes of Pete Lingle's brandy still hung in his head. He still had the use of quarters in Old Bedlam, for Colonel Long still wanted him as Chief of Scouts. In some ways it wasn't a bad idea, except for the fact that Miles still liked the more solitary life of a buffalo runner. But then the buffalo were doomed. Already the great herds were shrinking at an incredible rate as hunters infested the plains from Texas clear up into Indian country in the Dakotas.

He stabled the bay and unsaddled him, then walked toward his quarters, ready for a hot meal, a few soothing drinks, and a good night's sleep. Maybe the liquor would help him forget Lorena Carlisle, at least for a while. Nothing else seemed able to do it, and then in the morning she was always there again in his waking thoughts.

A young officer came out of the quarters as Miles walked along the path. "Mister Flint, sir," he said. "Colonel Long asked to see you as soon as you returned. He's in his quarters now."

"Thanks," said Miles. "I'll see him tomorrow."

The officer hesitated. "He seemed to think it was important, Mister Flint. I'll take your gear into your room."

Miles nodded. He handed the gear and his Sharps rifle to the shavetail and walked across the corner of the wet parade ground toward the misty lights of the colonel's quarters, glancing toward the quarters that had been occupied by Jonas and Lorena. The place was dark. He had half hoped she might still be there, but he knew without asking that she was not. He rapped on the colonel's door and entered without waiting for a reply.

Long looked up from his desk. He pushed aside a letter he had been writing. "By God," he said. "You took your time about it, Miles! I expected you back no later than yesterday."

Miles smiled wearily. "Am I under your orders, Colonel? Maybe I've been conscripted and don't know it."

Long shook his head. "Help yourself to the spirits," he said. He shoved a cigar box across the table and waited until Miles had his glass and his smoke. Miles sagged back in the chair and rested his head on the back of it, blowing a languorous cloud of smoke toward the ceiling.

Long leaned forward. "Before he left for the Bozeman, Carlisle hired himself another scout."

"Tell me who," said Miles politely.

"Bat Batteau," said the officer.

"Jesus Christ!" exploded Miles.

"I wholeheartedly agree," said Long dryly.

Miles looked at the officer in complete disbelief. "Didn't you tell him about Bat?"

"No. Bat was camped just off the post. I've barred him from the post proper. Bat must have gone out to the trail herd camp and sold Carlisle a real bill of goods."

"Amen to that," said Miles.

"Bat hates your guts. Maybe he did it just to make you look bad."

Miles shook his head. "There's more to it than that. When would Bat Batteau get up the guts to scout in Sioux territory? Carlisle would be better off with no scout at all."

Long sat down and rested his elbows on the desk. "The last time Bat was hanging around here he was telling the story of how he killed the famous Sioux war-chief Bull-over-the-Hill in ferocious hand-to-hand combat."

"It was bull over the hill all right," said Miles.

Long sipped his liquor as his calm eyes studied Miles. "Bat has his famous Ree scouts with him, too—Horns-in-Front, Goose, Stabbed, and Bear's Eyes, to name a few."

Miles drained his glass and went to get a refill. "Jesus God," he said fervently, rolling his eyes upward. "Now I've heard everything. *Everything!*"

Long nodded. "That is why I wanted to see you. Carlisle needs all the help he can get. A man like Batteau can lead him into trouble instead of keeping him out of it. At the sight of one Sioux scout Batteau is likely to pull foot and stand not on the order of his going, and Carlisle cannot possibly get by without a top-grade scout. Such as you, Miles."

"Such as me," said Miles. "You know how I stand on the matter."

Long nodded again. "You really wanted to go, Miles," he said.

"What makes you say that?"

"It's the woman, isn't it?"

The wind had shifted, driving the rain across the post. It pattered against the windows, and the wind moaned softly down the chimney.

"You don't have to answer that," said the colonel.

"I don't intend to," said Miles.

"Perhaps you left the trail herd because of her. No matter. Carlisle needs you now. She needs you now."

"You might be talking me into my own death, Dent," said Miles quietly.

Denton Long smiled. "Who ever talked you into *anything*, Miles?" He leaned forward again. "God knows I can use you here. God knows I don't want you to ride to your own death. But God also knows your mind as no one else does. The decision is yours." The officer got up and walked to the window, looking out across the rainswept parade ground. "An early storm," he said. "Coming from the north. Carlisle's bunch will be feeling this tonight."

"What would you do, Dent, if you were in my position?" said Miles.

"I am *not* in your position, Miles."

"Don't fence with me, Dent."

The officer turned. "If I loved that woman, as I think you do, no matter what the circumstances or what the eventual consequences, I would be riding toward the Bozeman Trail with her."

There was a long silence from Miles. He drained the glass. "Can I borrow a horse? My bay is tired."

"He'll be all right tomorrow."

Miles looked at him. "I'm leaving tonight. Now. I'll lead the bay. I can leave your issue mount at the stagecoach swing station at Muddy Creek. It can be brought back behind the next coach coming east."

Long shook his head. "I'll give you one of my own horses, Miles. Keep it. I owe it to you many times over. Anything else?"

Miles shook his head.

"Carlisle stocked up on a case or two more of split-breech Remingtons, an extra Colt or Remington six-shooter for each man. He hired more men. Men anxious to get to the goldfields but afraid to try it alone or in small parties. He's got a good outfit, Miles. There's a long, long outside chance he might make it."

Miles stood up and relighted his cigar. "The man of destiny," he said. He spat into the garboon.

It wasn't until he hit the ruts of the Bozeman not far from the crossing of Brown's Creek that Miles saw the telltale streamer of dust against the sky to the south. Beck Sterret

67

had been pushing the herd hard as long as there was plenty of grazing, water, and a good road.

Miles unsaddled the bay and picketed both horses in the bottoms. He started a fire and brewed coffee. Ernie Masland would appreciate having a fire when he reached the creek, provided Beck Sterret would agree to stop there.

Miles stayed in the cover of the brush, watching the rutted trail winding up over the southern ridge. Suddenly a horseman appeared, sitting a fine white horse, holding a hand across his eyes in approved scout fashion, studying the creek bottoms. The wind made sport with the thrums of his white buckskin jacket. Miles lazily rolled over and took his binoculars from his saddlebag. He adjusted them and studied the man on the ridge. He grinned as he saw the intricate beadwork of the scout's buckskin jacket and the scalp hair along the sides of the leggings. Oversized thrums hung from the sleeves of the jacket and fringed the yoke of the garment. There was enough beadwork on the jacket to turn a bullet. The wind whipped the scout's long black hair from beneath the brim of his white hat. Once again the scout peered beneath his hand, rising in his stirrups as he did go.

"Gawdamighty," said Miles in awe. "Bat Batteau! The Scout of the Great Plains! The slayer of Bull-over-the-Hill! In person tonight! One performance only!"

Bat rode down the ridge followed by half a dozen riders. They were Arikaras—small, wiry, dirty, and careless in their dress, which was half Indian and half white. They wore their thick black hair combed fully to one side or the other as was their custom.

The dust was rising thickly from behind the ridge. Bat was too damned close to the herd to do effective scouting, and in addition there likely wasn't a hostile Indian within fifty miles. Further, if Bat was scouting, his Rees should have been no less than half a day's ride ahead of the herd. Jonas Carlisle had been gulled by one of the worst hypocrites west of the Mississippi.

A heavy-set horseman topped the ridge and rode down after the "scouts." It was Jonas Carlisle. A moment later Beck Sterret appeared, riding in the deceptively loose fashion of a Texan.

Bat turned in his saddle fifty yards from the creek. "All clear, Mister Carlisle!" he yelled. "Ain't hide nor ha'r of any hostiles. Seen a little smoke awhile back, but we scouted it. A handful of hostiles, but they run when they seen me and the Rees." He laughed uproariously. "They wanted no part of *us!*"

Miles shook his head. Likely a grass fire. Miles had seen

one several miles back, staining the clear air. Bat was playing his role to the hilt.

The Rees crowded toward the creek, jabbering amongst themselves. Miles could have killed every one of them before he was even seen. The Rees stopped short when they saw the picketed horses. The wind fanned the fire, and the smoke drifted toward Bat, Jonas, and Beck. Jonas turned quickly in his saddle. Bat jerked his carbine free from its fancy beaded sheath.

Miles stood up leisurely. "It's all right, Bat," he said dryly. "Like you said: Ain't hide nor ha'r of any hostiles."

Bat's bearded face seemed to go out of focus, changing from a massive grin into a look of pure hate. "Flint," he said. "What the hell are yuh doin' here?"

Miles felt for a cigar. "Colonel Long said Mister Carlisle needed a scout."

"I'm scoutin' for Mister Carlisle!" snapped Bat.

Miles nodded. "That's what the colonel told me."

Beck Sterret shifted in his saddle. His look was cold as compared to the hot hatred on Batteau's face.

The first of the cattle had topped the ridge, bawling as they picked up the odor of the water. Ernie Masland's chuck-wagon lurched into sight and rolled down toward the campsite.

Batteau flushed darkly. "Long said you was goin' to scout for him."

Miles lighted the cigar and looked over the flame at Bat. "He must have come out from the post to you to tell you that. It's a cinch *you* never came onto the post to tell him."

"What does that mean?" said Jonas.

Miles fanned out the match. "That's between Bat and me," he said.

"Bat knows this country better than any scout in the business," said Jonas.

"Did he tell you that?" said Miles.

Jonas narrowed his eyes. "Come to think of it, he did."

Beck Sterret leaned forward in his saddle. "Bat says we can get through all right."

"When were you last up that way, Bat?" said Miles.

Bat's green eyes shifted uncertainly. He wiped his mouth with the back of a dirty hand. "The hostiles been quiet all summer. The Bozeman is like a country lane. Maybe quieter."

"The time to look for trouble is when they are quiet," said Miles.

"I got good scouts," said Bat. "Ain't no hostiles goin' to fool them."

"Rees," said Miles contemptuously. "Corn Indians."

Jonas lighted a cigar. "Bat says the Rees are the best scouts and fighters on the Plains," he said.

"And you believed him," said Miles. "My God!"

Bat shifted angrily in his saddle. "By God, Flint," he said, "yuh ain't the only judge of Indians in this country."

"Those Rees won't get within ten miles of a Sioux or Cheyenne, and you know it, Bat. Stop kidding and be honest for once in your life."

"Why, yuh dirty . . ."

Miles took the cigar from his mouth. "Now, Bat," he said quietly.

Bat shut up. He looked angrily at the two other men. "As long as he ain't part of this outfit, we got to listen to *him?*"

Beck Sterret spat. "Not far's I'm concerned," he drawled. "Like I said befoah: All them Indians want is sugah, tobaccy, whiskey, and wo-haw. A taste of powdersmoke will drive 'em off."

The mass of the herd was pouring down the slope toward the creek. Beck began to fashion a smoke. "With scouts out ahead, the herd bunched, every man riding the flanks, and the drag armed with them britchloader rifles, we can drive this herd plumb to Hudson's Bay."

Bat slapped a dirty hand on his buckskin-clad thigh. "Well spoken, Sterret! We'll work well together, you and me!"

There was a moment's pause. The glacial gray eyes studied Bat Batteau. "You do *yore* job, Mistah Batteau," said Beck softly, "and I'll do *mine*. One difference is thet I'll damned well see to it thet you do yores."

"Beck," said Jonas. "That's no way to talk to Bat."

Beck kneed his gray away from the others. "Far's I'm concerned," he said flatly, "we can do without these buckskin boys and theah fightin' talk. But if yuh want to pay them wages, Mistah Carlisle, and have them eat up food the trail drivers can use, it's all right with me. Just keep them out of my way and the way of the herd." He spurred his horse and rode swiftly toward the herd.

Bat whistled softly. "What's in his craw?" he said.

One of the Studebakers topped the ridge and rolled downslope. The wind fluttered a dress. Miles raised his eyes. It was Lorena, and suddenly the world seemed all right again, at least for a little while. Miles looked at Ernie Masland. "Here's your fire, Ernie!" he called out. "Ready to cook coffee and grub."

"*Gracias,* Miles!" yelled the grinning cocinero. "Welcome home!"

"I'm not home yet," said Miles.

Jonas bit off part of the end of his cigar and spat it out. "What does that mean?" he said.

The Studebaker, followed by the others, was moving toward Jonas, Bat, and Miles. Lorena placed a hand across her eyes to shade them. She had seen Miles.

"You mean you'll ride with us, Miles?" said Jonas.

Miles looked up at him. "I'd like to," he said. "If you don't mind."

Jonas rubbed his thick beard. "I can certainly use you."

The Studebaker rolled up and stopped beside Jonas. Lorena smiled a little uncertainly at Miles.

"Yuh got scouts, Mister Carlisle," said Bat. He glanced at Lorena.

Jonas nodded. "But no meat hunter. Miles, will you take that job at least?"

Miles did not dare look at Lorena. "Glad to, Jonas," he said.

That night the wind laughed deep in its throat as it swept across the hills, coming from the north, from the Big Horn and Powder River country. The wind knew a great deal not vouchsafed to puny mortals. Perhaps it was better that they did not know.

CHAPTER EIGHT

Bat Batteau continued leading after Miles Flint rejoined the trail herd, throwing out a screen of his Rees. Bat put on a great show as long as Miles Flint went on his solitary way hunting for the trail drivers. Bat was quite sure that there wasn't a strong hostile party within miles, at least not strong enough to attack the trail drivers and their "britchloader" rifles. The Rees would leave camp at dawn, riding like the wind, to put a few miles between them and the slowly moving herd, and then they'd find a shady draw or a clump of willows along a stream course to rest and play at knucklebones until it was time to move on again ahead of the herd. Naturally they didn't get *too* far ahead, for they liked the thought of the tough, alert Texans and their "britchloader" rifles being fairly close at hand in case there *were* any hostiles within shooting distance. Bat managed to sleep off many a hangover during the day while his Rees kept an eye on the herd rather than on the surrounding country. If nothing else, Bat had thoroughly sold himself and his Rees to Jonas Carlisle.

The country ahead of the herd seemed empty, indeed, except for an occasional hawk drifting against the clear sky with motionless wings in the dry wind, or the sudden movement of pronghorn antelope, or clumsily running buffalo, moving with deceptive speed away from the approaching herd.

Miles Flint did his job, at times being a full day or more ahead of the herd, waiting for them at some watering place with a load of meat, or at times hanging the meat to be picked up later and then moving on by himself. The country seemed empty, and maybe it was, but there was an uneasy feeling within him, particularly when he approached the Pumpkin Buttes country, where the Bozeman trended northwest to follow the Dry Fork of the Powder. The country was closing in on the Bozeman, and what was behind those hills only God, and the Teton Sioux, knew.

The passage had been too easy thus far, too quiet. Miles could use some of Bat's Rees now, to poke into those draws and mottes, to scale the bluffs and look for any sign. Several times in his lone ride far ahead of the herd he had found telltale dark patches along the Bozeman—blackened earth, still coated with ashes beaten down by the rains, and pieces of rust-scaled wagon iron lying amongst them. Lorena Carlisle could hardly miss seeing them. Several times he passed crude crosses, with the names and dates almost illegible, placed close to the trail. Likely few, or perhaps none of them had died natural deaths.

He saw the buffalo one afternoon when he was perhaps half a day's ride ahead of the herd. They had moved out of a deep draw, moving into the freshening north wind, drifting slowly toward the shallow creek some miles ahead. The creek was marked by a scraggly dark line of willows, beyond which there was a low line of rounded hills. Fresh buffalo hump would go good that night with some of Jonas Carlisle's choice liquor. Miles led the bay into a shallow draw and picketed him, taking his rifle and other gear with him as, hatless, he worked his way up a slope stippled with soapweed. He fitted the 'scope to the rifle and thrust it between two clumps, resting it on the crotch of his shooting sticks. The nearest buffalo were about two hundred and fifty yards away, with the wind blowing almost directly toward Miles. He tossed out his lighted cigar butt and watched the smoke rise, then waver with the wind.

Miles selected a big cow at the downwind edge of the herd. The Sharps roared, and when the smoke cleared Miles saw that the cow was still on her feet, walking unsteadily away from the herd. Suddenly she jerked spasmodically and went down on her foreknees, the blood gushing from her nose and mouth. A bull raised his head and sniffed the air. The sun glinted from his horns. Miles reloaded. He needed only a few carcasses, enough to pick the select cuts of meat. He drove his second slug into a young cow. She crumpled instantly. His third shot missed because of a sudden gust of wind.

Miles reloaded and rested his chin on the butt of the rifle, idly waiting to see what the herd would do. He had enough meat. The herd was restless now, sniffing the air, raising their heads. Some of them wandered over to the dead animals, sniffing at them, hooking at them with their horns. Dust rose and drifted with the wind as some of the bulls pawed the ground and snorted. They were not quite ready to panic, but they were getting more restless. Miles suddenly narrowed his eyes. There was a whitish blob in the center of the small herd, as though a beef cow had somehow gotten mixed up with them. The buffalo moved about, shifting in front of the whitish blob, so that Miles couldn't get a clear sight of what it was.

Miles reached for his binoculars and sighted them on the herd, focusing to bring them in more sharply. In the shimmering heat the buffalo looked as if they were suspended above the dry ground. Miles focused on the whitish blob, and his heart skipped a beat, thudding erratically against his ribs. He hurriedly wiped the sweat from his forehead and wiped the misted eyepieces on his shirt. He focused again. The whitish mass stood out clearly. A young bull with a shaggy, dirty pelt of creamy coloration. "By God," said Miles under his breath. "A sure enough snow-back!"

He lowered the glasses and closed his eyes. Maybe he was seeing things. Few hunters, or any men, white or Indian, had likely ever seen a white, or albino, buffalo. Maybe the odds were one in a million, or perhaps less. Miles carefully cleaned the lens and the eyepieces, then adjusted the glasses again. His heart leaped again. He was right! The sun shone clearly on the dirty, matted hide. *Begod, it was a snow-back!*

The wind shifted again, then died away. The cigar smoke wafted straight up into the air. Miles placed the glasses to one side and took up the Sharps. His right hand closed about the small of the stock. He didn't want to hole that precious hide in the wrong place. The young bull turned and looked directly at Miles, as though feeling those keen gray eyes upon him. The Sharps pushed back hard against Miles as smoke and flame spat from the big muzzle. The thunder of the heavy gun report rolled along the face of the low hills and died away.

Miles raised his head from the 'scope and lowered the smoking rifle. The snow-back was down, flat on its side, with blood masking the whitish face. Miles snatched up the glasses and

73

focused them on the bull. "Begod," he said incredulously. "Right in the eye."

The herd was moving swiftly in their jerky up-and-down gallop, the cows and calves in the center, the bulls flanking, slamming into the rising wind, the ground shaking beneath their hooves, leaving their dead behind them on the blood-stained grass. In a few minutes they had topped a swale and were gone from sight, but the ground still trembled faintly beneath the pounding of their hooves and the dust wreathed back on the wind.

Miles reloaded the hot Sharps. He removed the 'scope and slid it into its leather case. He slung rifle and 'scope to the saddle and led the bay toward the dead buffalo. There was enough meat, counting the albino, to keep the drivers happy for a few days. They never seemed to get tired of fresh buffalo hump and steak.

He led the bay near the white bull and then stood studying the dead buffalo. It was a bull about two years old. The hide was far whiter then he had expected it to be, even though it was matted with filth and burrs, stuck with grass and dried dung. It was a much better hide than old Jules Beque had once gotten on the Cimarron. That had been more of a silver gray in color, whited tips on the end of black hair. This one was almost pure white with a creamy tinge to it, not as dark as a claybank.

Miles honed his skinning knife and crescent knife on his belt steel and then carefully set to work, his loaded rifle close to hand and his eyes flicking up regularly, scanning the country on all sides. The reports of the rifle could have been heard for miles, and the trail herd was still a long way off, too far for the drivers to be of any help to Miles should he be attacked. There wasn't much chance that Bat Batteau and his Rees would be close to Miles, as they should have been.

He had no pritchell stick with which to prop the bull on his back, so he fastened his reata to the right legs and fastened the other end to the saddlehorn, leading the bay back until the bull rose flat on its back. "Stand," he said to the bay. The bay would not move.

He slit the thick hide from beneath the lower jaw, working along the neck, constantly renewing the edge on his skinning knife so as not to tear the hide, until he had worked down the belly to the tail. He thrust the skinning knife into the belly meat and drew out the crescent knife, scanning the terrain as he did so. High in the sky there appeared what looked to be scraps of charred paper being driven by the wind; the ravens were already gathering. He worked steadily and surely with the keen-edged crescent knife, cutting around the thick neck,

74

taking the ears but leaving the skin of the head. Then he began the dirty, greasy work of loosening the hide from the carcass.

Flies arrived, crawling and swarming, and time and time again he had to stop to brush them away from his sweating face while they crawled irritatingly over his greasy, bloody hands and naked forearms. He kicked the hide as far as he could under one side of the carcass, then whistled to the bay. The bay moved toward Miles, letting the reata slacken until the carcass rolled sluggishly and fell over. Miles worked under the heavy back until the hide was free from the backbone. Ordinarily he would have fastened the reata to the neck and peeled off the hide by having the bay pull on the reata, but he might have torn the precious albino hide, and this above all he did not want to do.

He heaved the hide over and worked it free from the hot, bloody carcass. The green hide weighed all of eighty or ninety pounds. It was a beauty, free of bare spots and blemishes. Miles lighted a cigar to get the stink of the carcass out of his nostrils and to drive away some of the persistent flies. He began to cut loose the select meat he wanted, cutting free the *depouille* or back fat, and placing it on a square of canvas he took from his cantle roll. He slashed out the tough gristly skin between the prongs of the tightly closed jaws, then pulled the thick tongue through the opening and cut it off. He worked on the hump, cutting down each side of the shoulders and then chopping through the hump ribs with his heavy, brass-backed bowie knife. He cut loose the larger bones for the delicious marrow in them, better than any butter to a veteran plainsman.

He slit open the belly and felt about in the hot, steaming interior until he located the saddlebag-sized liver, which he cut loose and pulled out. He opened the gallbladder, then cut loose a sliver of the hot liver and sprinkled it with gall. He hadn't eaten all day long. He munched Indian-fashion on the tidbit with relish while he removed the heart, kidneys, and intestines, pulling the slippery, greasy intestines through his strong fingers to clean out the body wastes, then knitting the long slippery tubes into a loopy chain.

Miles stood up to ease his back and get his nose away from the stench. He wiped the sweat from his face and reached for the cigar, which he had placed on one upthrust hoof. His hand stopped in midair. Not thirty feet from him a young Sioux buck sat his paint pony on a low knoll. There was no expression on the buck's painted face. His trade musket, studded with brass tacks, was lying in the crook of his left arm, the muzzle pointing directly at Miles.

Miles was too far from the Sharps to make a break for it. He had shoved his holstered Remington pistol around to

75

the middle of his back to keep it out of the way, and the flap was buttoned down. At that short distance the soft ball of the big-bored musket could tear off half his head or gut him as he had gutted the buffalo bull. Damn his carelessness! He should have known better. Why hadn't the bay warned him of the buck's approach? He turned to look for the bay, half expecting to hear the raucous bellow of the trade musket. His guts seemed to turn over. The bay had drifted not far from where another buck sat, his blanket hanging over his naked thighs, the sun shining on his white pipe-bone breast-piece, his long-barreled flintlock rifle casually aimed toward Miles.

Something warned Miles, an insistent needle in the back of his mind. He glanced to the right. Another buck stood on the ground near one of the dead cows, his eyes on Miles, and the black eye of a Jenks carbine studying Miles as well.

Miles looked at the first buck. *"How kola,"* he said stupidly. He raised his bloody hands, palms outward toward the buck in the sign of peace. There was no movement, no change of expression on the buck's face. Miles felt the cold sweat run down his body. Indians hated buffalo runners with a vengeance for killing far, far more of the shaggies than they needed for meat, leaving the good meat to rot on the prairie while they took away only the green hides. The whole economy, indeed the very life of these people depended on *Pte,* the good buffalo. They did not waste a scrap of *Pte.* Everything was used. Meat, sinews, hide, horns, hooves, bones, guts, and blood. Everything but the snort.

I am going to die, thought Miles incredulously. I am going to die, perhaps suddenly, perhaps slowly, but I am going to die. This can't happen to me, Miles Flint. This must be someone else standing here, smeared with buffalo blood and fat, someone else who is going to die.

The buck on the knoll kneed his horse closer to Miles. Young as he was, he wore an erect eagle feather in his hair indicating that he had killed an enemy after striking coup on him. The feather was notched twice, indicating that he had been twice wounded in the fight.

They were playing with Miles now, as a cat plays with a mouse, knowing full well he was powerless. He looked out of the corners of his eyes at the folded hide of the snow-back. Only the inner, flesh-coated side of the hide showed. Miles took in a deep breath and walked casually as he could toward the hide. He heard the sharp snick-snick of a rifle hammer being full-cocked behind him. He reached down and suddenly jerked at the greasy edge of the hide, twisting it so that it unrolled outer side upward, with the sun slanting fully down on it, revealing the dirty cream white of the pelt.

There were three startled cries. Three brown hands covered open mouths in sheer awe. The bucks stared at the hide with wide eyes. This was medicine! This was big medicine indeed!

Miles raised his head and looked directly at each of them in turn, trying to keep fear from showing on his face.

Slowly, foot by foot, the two closest bucks retreated. They suddenly flung themselves on their ponies. The three Sioux savagely quirted their ponies and raced from the wide hollow, and in a few minutes they plunged out of sight into a brushy draw.

Miles dropped to one knee, then sat down suddenly. He felt his guts roil and the sour taste of bile in the back of his throat. His legs were as weak as water. He crawled to his rifle and used it as a prop to get up onto his feet. He looked to the south. The sun glinted on the great spreading horns of the cattle as they streamed down a ridge in a long, sinuous line. Seven riders were flung out ahead of the herd in a fast-riding crescent heading toward Miles and his kill. It was Bat Batteau and his Rees, hard at work, scouting so close to the herd that the smell and sound of it would be sure to stampede any small parties of hostiles.

The six Rees seemed to scent the buffalo meat like coyotes. They drove their lathered ponies full tilt across the rolling ground, lashing them with their quirts, yipping tremulously in their excitement, while Bat Batteau, *the* Scout of the Plains, rode along behind them laughing uproariously. He could afford to laugh, for the day had been a safe and easy one and now good buffalo hump was in the offing.

Miles wiped the grease and blood from his arms and hands. He swept the flies from his face and wiped the skinning knives on the carcass, sheathing them in their oiled leather cases. Swiftly he rolled up the hide, the white pelt inside, securing it with thrums from his saddlebag. He covered the hide with a blanket and slung it from his saddle. These damned Rees and Bat Batteau would surely know the value of a snow-back pelt if none of the others did. Men had been murdered for the possession of such hides.

The Rees leaped from their ponies, screaming, ripping out their knives to slash wildly at the nearest cow, careless of cutting buffalo or the flesh of their mates as they sliced into the big belly, hunting with bloody hands for the huge liver, the steam from the guts streaming up about their painted faces and making them look like demons straight from hell.

Miles picked up his rifle and led the bay away from the carcasses. Jonas Carlisle and Lorena were riding toward the group.

Bat Batteau dismounted, exaggerated thrums fluttering in the wind. The sun glistened on the crusted beadwork of his buckskins. "Good huntin', eh, pardner!" he yelled at Miles, a wide grin creasing his bearded face. "Guess the hostiles won't bother you with me and the Rees scoutin' ahead, hey?"

Miles lighted a fresh cigar and fanned out the match, watching Lorena as she rode her mare sidesaddle with expert skill, riding habit shirt pulled up enough to reveal the tiniest of riding boots.

Bat eyed the carcasses. "Where's the hide from that one?" he asked Miles, pointing to the skinned bull.

Miles shrugged. "Figured I might need a good buffalo coat before we reached the Gallatin."

"I thought you knew your business," said Bat. "That bull can't be mor'n two years old. A four- or five-year-old bull woulda been better. Thicker and hairier."

Miles could smell the stench rising from his sweating body, and he didn't want Lorena to get scent of it. He swung up on the bay.

"Good hunting, eh, Miles?" said Jonas. "I fancy some hump this night."

"Have Bat send one of his Rees for one of the wagons," said Miles. "I'll ride on to the creek and get a fire started for Ernie. The Rees can earn their keep by cutting out the meat."

"Good thinking," agreed Jonas.

Miles's eyes met those of Lorena. There was a faint hurt look in them. She looked away. They rarely saw each other now except at a distance.

Bat placed a moccasined foot on the biggest cow and watched three of the Rees expertly skinning a smaller cow. It was one thing they were good at. "I was tellin' Flint here it was good that me and the Rees was out here watchin' for hostiles so's he could hunt in peace, Mister Carlisle," he said.

Miles blew out a smoke ring. *"Heyoka,"* he said in guttural Sioux. He tipped his dusty hat to Lorena and touched the bay with his heels, riding swiftly toward the distant creek bottoms several miles away.

"What did he mean, Bat?" said Lorena.

Bat's green eyes seemed to be boring a smoking hole in the middle of Miles's broad, buckskin-clad back.

"Bat?" said Lorena.

He turned slowly, the look of hate still on his face, although he tried to bury it with a quick smile. "It's a little joke amongst us plainsmen, Mis' Carlisle. It ain't exactly fittin' for a lady's ears."

Bat Batteau wasn't exactly right. *Heyoka* in the Sioux tongue means "joker."

78

CHAPTER NINE

It was dry and hot in the dark valley of the Dry Fork, and an uneasiness hung low in the atmosphere. The wind had died away hours back after another exceptionally hot day. Perhaps it was too be a mild fall after all. Miles Flint rode the tired sorrel through the clinging darkness toward the camp of the trail herd somewhere southeast of him. The sky had been clear and starlit when he had left the crossing of the Powder River just before dusk. A three-day scout north of the slow-moving herd had been fruitless. He had not seen a sign of a hostile, although once there had been a faint wraith of smoke rising through the haze of late autumn somewhere far up the valley of the Powder. It could have been a grass fire. There hadn't been enough of it to indicate a large camp of Sioux.

The overcast seemed thicker. There was a faint, insistent flickering along the western horizon etching the fanged hills. The sheet lightning grew in intensity as he rode, and the quiet air grew more oppressive. Faintly, ever so faintly, the Thunder People rolled their drums. The humidity seemed to rise.

Miles stood up in his stirrups. He should have seen or heard the longhorns by now. If the lightning and thunder increased, the cattle might stampede. There had been no stampeding after that fateful afternoon on a fork of the Smoky Hill, and that had been only part of the herd. It was a day Miles would remember bitterly for the rest of his life.

The night grew blacker as the eerie lightning became brighter, etching itself in staghorn fashion across the sky. The thunder pealed louder and louder through the valleys and along the line of hills. Suddenly, far ahead of him down a long slope, Miles saw a creek bed marked by a line of willows and by the dark shapes of thousands of cattle. In the instant of bluish, uncanny light Miles saw that many of the beeves were on their feet; others getting up in the quick, almost catlike movement of a longhorn, from lying down to upright on their legs, without the double movement of other cattle or of buffalo.

Suddenly there was an intense electrical discharge spanning the width of the valley, splitting the charged air right over the herd. The herd began to move slowly at a walk and as darkness plunged down again Miles saw an eerie sight. Almost instantaneously on every horntip of the three thousand or so steers appeared a ball of dull, phosphorescent light. It was foxfire, or St. Elmo's fire, sometimes called will-o-the-wisp. Suddenly it appeared on the ears of the tired, nervous sorrel. The dull balls of fire on the thousands of horntips could be plainly seen in the thick darkness. They were moving slowly toward Miles. There was a faint suggestion of wind moving the heavy air in the valley, and the smell and sound of the herd came to Miles.

As quick as the crack of doom a tremendous flash of staghorn lightning forked across the herd of longhorns, and the flaming tongues seemed almost to touch the backs of the cattle. A crashing of what seemed like heavy artillery followed on the flailing heels of the lightning, and then the herd broke in the direction of the lone horseman. Pounding hooves made the ground tremble, and the clacking of horn against horn was a terrifying sound. Then the sluice gates of the sky opened on the valley of the Dry Fork, and the rain came down in almost impenetrable sheets. The lightning split a fiery path through the deluge to reveal the herd pounding madly up the valley, eyes wide and staring, horns wet and slick.

Miles reined in the sorrel and turned him, driving the steel into his flanks. He knew the rules in a stampede. He had learned them well enough riding with Nelson Story. Hang with the cattle. Trust your horse. But the sorrel was almost dead beat. The ground was already turning slick, and the way was up the slope, with the fresh cattle, running almost as fast as a slow horse, whiplashed by the lightning, thunder, and fear itself.

Miles did not look back. He lay low alongside the sorrel's neck, trusting to God the sorrel had some reserve left. The sound of the pounding hooves and clacking horns came clearly to him in the intervals between the crackling lightning and roaring thunder. His hat flew off and hung at the back of his neck. There was nothing to do but run.

The sorrel was slowing down. Miles shot a look back over his shoulder and his heart skipped a beat. Already a crescent horn of the herd was creeping up on his right flank, gaining ground inch by inch. There was something else. Two horsemen were riding with incredible daring and skill against the leaders of the crescent horn to turn them in on the herd, to mill it, to force it to turn itself into a great revolving mass until it could be quieted down. Only the best could do it.

The horn began to turn a little. One of the horseman jerked his six-shooter free and fired it, driving his horse almost directly into the streaming-wet flanks of the leaders. Miles thought he could clear the crescent. He laid the steel to the sorrel. The sorrel jerked spasmodically and then went down. Miles just managed to kick free from the stirrups and land running on his feet, knowing all the time he had only seconds to live.

The lead horseman swung toward Miles, kicking out a stirrup. Miles braced himself, trying to keep his eyes away from the nearest cattle. He trust a foot into the dangling stirrup and gripped the rider's broad gunbelt, letting the momentum of the horse carry him up and behind the rider.

The second rider smashed against the head of the herd, slowly turning them. Miles's savior rode up a rise and drew rein. "Off!" he said flatly. It was then Miles knew that it was Beck Sterret. Sterret reloaded his pistol as Miles swung down.

"Gracias," said Miles.

"Por nada," said the Texan.

Miles wiped the rain from his face. He looked up at the hard face of the trail boss. "One thing," he said. "Did you know it was me?"

Sterret kneed his horse away from Miles. "You figger it out, Yank," he said. "I got my job to do." He was gone, racing down the slope, seemingly part of the horse itself, to drive into the leaders of the herd. Blackness fell and with it a smashing downpour of icy rain. When lightning flicked across the valley Miles could see the herd slowly turning, but many longhorns had broken free from the herd and were pounding toward the distant hills. It would be hours, perhaps days before the trail herd could be formed again for the drive north.

Miles turned up his jacket collar. There was no use looking for the sorrel. His smashed body would be part and parcel of the trampled, muddy path of the stampeded herd. Miles walked up the slope, away from the stragglers of the herd and toward the creek. Every man would be out that wild night to save the herd.

The day dawned clear and cold along the valley of the Dry Fork. Most of the herd had been penned against the distant hills, but far up and down the valley were the dotted shapes of stragglers. A wisp of smoke rose from the campfire, fired by the dry buffalo chips Ernie Masland carried in the "cooney" slung beneath the chuckwagon. Now and then a herder rode his worn-out horse toward the creek, grabbed a mug of Arbuckle's, roped a fresh horse, and was on his way again in a matter of minutes. A trail herder could always catch up on his sleep in the winter.

Jonas Carlisle returned to the camp in the gathering dusk. "Did you see Bat and his Rees, Miles?" was his first question as he swung down stiffly from his gray.

Miles shook his head. He had finished cleaning his Sharps, which he had left behind in the charge of Ernie Masland when he had gone ahead on his lonely scout. "All I saw was buffalo crap and a little smoke up the valley of the Powder," he said dryly.

Jonas eased his crotch and helped himself to a cup of coffee. "Bat said he'd join you up north. I told him not to stay away more then a day, Miles."

Miles leaned the Sharps against a tree. An odd thought had come to him. Miles had carried the green albino hide with him on his three-day scout. It had been one of the reasons why he had asked Carlisle's permission to scout ahead on his own. In a hidden clearing in the timber crowning a hill not far from the Powder he had firmly staked out the green hide, hair side down, and had covered it with arsenic to kill insects. The days had been hot and sunny. Miles had figured that by the time he returned to the hide it would be fully dry, a flint hide, weighing about half the weight of a green hide and ready for transport. That hide was almost worth its weight in silver. Bat Batteau would have known that, if he had known or suspected that Miles had killed a snow-back.

"But you never saw him, eh, Miles?" said Jonas.

"It's a big country," said Miles.

"Maybe he ran into the Sioux."

Miles grinned as he helped himself to coffee. "Not likely," he said.

"I know you have no use for him," said Jonas testily. "But I had to take what I could get when you backed out on me."

Miles placed the cup on a rock and looked up at the trail driver. "You would have been better off without him," he said. "And I did not back out on you."

Jonas's face worked. He was tired, not used to riding all night and the next day rounding up stray cattle like the hard-butted Texas corrida. "Damn it all, man," he said. "Do you have to have that damned chip on your shoulder all the time?"

Miles stood up. "Only when I'm crowded," he said coldly.

"By God! If you work for me, you'll *learn* to be crowded!"

Cattle bawled along the creek, and the sound of singing came to the two men who faced each other, as the herders kept the longhorns calm. Ernie Masland looked at Jonas and Miles. He had never seen the two of them like this before, but nerves were taut. Jonas wasn't quite so sure of himself now that he was approaching the heart of Sioux country, and the stampede could have been disastrous.

"I don't work under those conditions," said Miles quietly.

"Are you God Almighty or something?" snapped Carlisle.

Miles picked up his rifle. "No," he said. "But I've had a bellyful of this bunch."

Beck Sterret was with the herd. He rode slowly toward the camp through the gathering dusk. Sterret had an uncanny knack of sensing trouble before it started or while it was in the process of getting started.

"You can leave, then," said Carlisle to Miles. "You're through."

Miles nodded. He carried the rifle to his gear and went to get the bay. His temper was hot and he wanted no further words with Jonas or, for that matter, with Beck Sterret. When he had roped and saddled the bay he saw Jonas and Beck riding back toward the herd.

He cursed himself for his hotheadedness. The trail driver needed him even more than he thought, for Bat Batteau and his Rees were more of a liability than an asset. He led the bay to his gear and fashioned cantle and pommel packs. Now and then he caught the eyes of Ernie Masland on him. He did not see Ernie walk to the Studebaker, nor did he see Lorena Carlisle mount her mare and ride into the darkness toward the gathering herd.

There was a faint trace of the new moon in the clear, cloudless sky when Miles swung up on the bay. He kneed him toward the creek. A horseman sat on the far side, smoking a cigar. The flare of the tip revealed the tired, bearded face of Jonas Carlisle. "Miles," he said. "I was a damned fool. On edge. We need you. Even Beck Sterret admits that."

Miles waded the bay through the shallow waters. "That should clinch it then," he said.

Jonas took the cigar from his mouth. "It will take us another day to get set to point them north, Miles. I don't know where Bat and his Rees are. See if you can find them. If not, I'll have to depend completely on you." His voice died away, and from the tone of it Miles knew how much Jonas Carlisle did depend on him.

"I owe you something," said Miles quietly. "I agreed to go along this time. I won't let you down. Come to think of it, I owe something to Beck Sterret as well."

"Such as?"

"My life," said Miles. "Say hello to Mrs. Carlisle for me. See you at the crossing of the Powder." He touched the bay with his spurs and rode off into the darkness.

"I'll be damned," said Jonas. He shoved back his hat. He rode to his wagon and dismounted stiffly.

Lorena looked up from her chair. "Well, Jonas?" she said.

He nodded. "You were right," he said. "A proud man, but a good man."

"You're tired. Beck is tired. Miles is tired. We're all tired."

He looked down at her and passed a hand across her dark hair. "We are not going back," he said.

She looked up at him. "I didn't mean that, Jonas. We're all in this to the end now."

Somewhere near the hills a coyote greeted the rising moon.

The rising moon was a pale wash in the eastern sky. The wind which had died away after sunset, rose again in the velvety darkness, moaning softly down the great valley of the Powder River, keening over the blackened ruins of Fort Reno, built by the Army in 1866 to protect the Bozeman Trail and burned by the Sioux in 1868, along with Forts Phil Kearny and C. F. Smith, further north on the Bozeman, leaving the route entirely without Army protection.

Miles Flint lay on his lean belly overlooking the river crossing. He had traveled at night, hiding by day, watching for Sioux sign without any luck until he had reached the crossing. Shortly before dusk he had seen a party of warriors cross the ford and disappear into the broken country to the north. There had been about a score of them, hardly enough to stop the trail herd. Later in the clinging darkness he had seen faint lights north of the Pumpkin Buttes, but they had soon vanished. There were no whites settled in that dangerous country, and a party of whites would hardly be stupid enough to show lights at night in the Powder River country. There could only be one source for those lights. This was the territory of Plenty Kills's powerful band of Oglalas.

The Sioux would not fight at night, but that didn't mean they would not scout at night. The crossing would be a dangerous one for the traveling herd. Stippled with scattered hemlock and yellow pine timber, thick with eroded draws and sharp ridges angling every whichway, it offered excellent concealment for large war parties. Miles led the bay down to the river, sniffing the air for the scent of burning buffalo chips or lathered ponies. The smell of the river came to him instead.

Miles crossed the river before the moon cast its lights upon the shallow, rippling waters. He rode through the dark timber and tethered the bay, climbing up the steep slope to pass into a clearing just being lighted by the moon. The pegged-out hide was still there. He knelt and examined it. It had cured well under the hot suns and was firm and dry. The rain that had deluged the Dry Fork country had evidently passed south of the Powder River crossing. Miles crimped it down the middle, lashed it together, and carried it to the bay. He folded a square of canvas about it and bound it tightly so that it could not be seen.

He led the bay back toward the crossing. He would have felt much better if he had seen the yellow lights of Fort Reno reflected across the rippling waters to meet the silvery path of the moonlight down the river center.

The moon was well up when he caught the sound of the herd. Beck Sterret must have been pushing them, riding through dusk and darkness to reach the Powder, after his loss of time with the stampede. The far side of the river was bathed in silvery light when Bat Batteau and his Rees appeared, clumped together. As fine a target as a group of Dog Soldiers would have wished for. Miles speculated idly that he could probably get all seven of them within three minutes.

Bat set his white horse at the river and splashed noisily across. Miles had seen neither hide nor hair of Bat and his Rees on his second scout to the Powder. Miles did not move from the log where he sat, watching Bat leave the river.

"Flint!" said Bat cheerfully. "All clear here?"

"You can see for yourself," said Miles dryly.

"Yeh. Well, how far you aimin' to go with Jonas?"

Miles felt for a cigar. "Maybe to the Gallatin."

Bat slid from his horse. "I heard talk around the camp last night that Jonas might cut you in on the herd if you was to go all the way."

"That's news to me," said Miles.

Bat shoved back his hat. "I'd like to get in on that," he said.

Miles lighted the cigar. "So?"

Bat squatted in front of Miles. "If you was to pull out in the next few days, say, or maybe go on just to the Buffalo, I could maybe make a deal like that myself with Jonas."

Miles studied the bearded scout. "Go on," he said mildly.

Bat took out a plug and bit off a chew. "Say you was gone, and me and the Rees was all he had to scout for him. Well, supposin' you had left, and we was in hostile country, and I told Jonas me and the Rees was pullin' out, like." He paused to work the chew into pliability. "Mebbe Jonas might, just *might*, mind you, cut *me* in on the herd like he might have thought of doin' for you. By Jesus, up on the Gallatin, with some of them cows, a man could make himself some *dinero*. A man can't go on forever livin' dangerously like this, and I ain't gettin' any younger, Flint, and sometimes I think my hair is goin' to get a lot looser if I keep foolin' around the Sioux. Not from old age, you understand. You see what I mean?"

Miles blew a smoke ring. "The way you're going about it,

85

Bat, you're safe enough. You're hardly ever out of range of those Remington rolling-blocks anymore."

Bat spat juicily and wiped his mouth on a sleeve. "Hell, them Sioux ain't likely to bother us this side of the Crazy Woman."

"How do you know that?" said Miles.

Bat shifted his green eyes. "Just guessin'," he said quickly.

"Where the hell have you been laying low these past days?"

Bat stood up. "What's that to you?" he said.

"All right to cross, Bat?" called out Jonas Carlisle from the other side of the river.

Bat shifted into character, striding to the edge of the river, his thrums fluttering in the night breeze. "Come on with them longhorns!" he yelled. "Water is shallow and bottom is hard. Ain't hide nor ha'r of a hostile for miles."

Miles walked to the edge of the river. Bat was shrewd enough to know that Miles wouldn't have been sitting there smoking if there were hostiles around. The herd was lowing and bellowing as it streamed toward the crossing. The moonlight was almost as bright as day now, and the crossing was safe enough. It might have been dangerous if it had rained as hard here as it had farther south. He saw the white tilts of the wagons moving toward the river and wondered how Lorena was. Rather than see her he walked to the bay and rode along the riverbank downstream from the noisy herd. Where had Bat been those few days? Probably holed up in the hills.

A mile from the crossing Miles drew rein and slid from the bay. He picked up his rifle and padded forward, keeping in the cover of the brush and trees, which were thinning out. He stayed behind cover and watched the broken hills. Something moved a little on one of them. Miles took out his field-glasses and focused on the hill. A wolf sat up there, watching the moonlight glittering on the water. Miles studied the face of the beast, and an instant before it moved out of sight he recognized it as a human face painted to resemble a wolf's. The pointed ears and long snout belonged to the wolf pelt that covered the scout. To the Sioux the words "scout" and "wolf" are interchangeable. Even as he scanned the moonlit hill he heard the howling of a wolf drifting down toward him. A moment later the haunting cry seemed to echo from the far side of the river and then again from the bottom timber further downstream.

Miles led the bay back toward the herd. He glanced over his shoulder and saw that the wolf had returned to the hillside. From its movements, in absolute mimicry of a wolf, it was hard to tell that it was indeed a man within that furry pelt.

Miles dropped a hand to his Sharps but thought better of it. There was no percentage in killing one scout.

The words of Bat Batteau came back to him as he neared the camp. "Hell, them Sioux ain't likely to bother us this side of the Crazy Woman." Had Bat been guessing *or did he know something?* Why had he been so anxious to get rid of Miles?

The herd was bedded down on the north side of the river. The smoke of the dying fires hung low in the bottoms. Now and then the mournful howling of wolves drifted down to the camp, and the Texans who rode night herd tightened their grips on the long-barreled Remingtons across their thighs. A wolf might slip in to rip at a young cow.

"Wolves is yella," said Bat Batteau as he emptied his whiskey glass and looked sideways at the half-full bottle on the folding table. "They won't bother them cows tonight."

Lorena Carlisle glanced at the lean man who sat just beyond the fire, his face alternately in darkness and in dim light as he drew on his cigar. Miles had hardly said a word since dinner.

Jonas Carlisle sipped at his whiskey. "Just the same," he said. "They don't seem much afraid of us. Actually it isn't really the wolves I'm thinking about. It's those human wolves somewhere beyond those hills that are bothering me."

Bat waved a careless hand. "Trust me and the Rees," he said. "You'll know when the Sioux are about. We done all right so far, ain't we? You ain't seen a one of 'em, have you?"

"No," admitted Jonas. "What's your opinion, Miles?"

Miles took the cigar from his mouth. "You should have your scouts at least half a day ahead of you from now on."

Bat shot Miles a killing glance. "That's my work, Flint," he said. *"I'm* doing the scouting for this drive."

Miles shrugged. "Then why don't you tell him those aren't wolves up in those hills?"

Bat flushed. He reached for the whiskey bottle.

Jonas stared at Miles. "If those aren't wolves, what are they?"

"Ask Bat," said Miles. "Like he said, *he's* doing the scouting."

Bat drained half the glass and wiped his mouth. "All right! All right!" he snapped. "Them are Sioux scouts up in them hills. I say the same thing about them I said about the wolves. They're yella, and besides, they won't bother us at night."

Lorena looked nervously toward the hills. "Will they watch us all night?"

"Don't worry none, ma'am," said Bat. "Me and the Rees will watch over yuh all right."

"Right from the camp." said Miles dryly. He stood up. "The day I killed those three buffalo there were Sioux scouts practically within sight of the herd, but Bat and his Rees didn't see them. A party of them crossed the Powder right here shortly before dusk. I saw lights north of the buttes after dusk, and there are no white men living there or even traveling there. Jonas, *we're riding right through the middle of them*. So far, perhaps out of pure luck but probably for some perverse reason of their own, they haven't hit you, *but they will when you least expect it!* Perhaps not a full-scale attack at first, but more of a whittling process until they've weakened you enough to stop you. Keep the herd bunched from now on. Don't let one driver get beyond rifle range of the next two drivers. Above all, if you must rely on Bat and his Rees, *make them get out where they belong!* They can't see, smell, or hear Sioux riding within sight of the herd. Right now they're absolutely useless and it's downright foolhardy to depend upon them."

Bat dropped his empty whiskey glass and stood up to face Miles. "What was that you said, Flint?" he said in a low tone.

"You heard me, Bat. By God, try to do your job! These people are depending on you, or doesn't that make any difference to you?" said Miles.

Jonas got to his feet. "Bat does his best, Miles," he said. "I want no trouble here."

Miles looked at Jonas. "You're paying this man for a job he isn't doing and never intended doing. At the first sign of real trouble he and his Rees will stampede worse than your longhorns did."

Bat shot a sideways glance at Jonas. "He's been drinkin' too much," he said.

"He's letting me do his work," said Miles. "He knows as long as I am out ahead of the herd I'm not going to allow you to run into the Sioux, but I can't cover all of the country between here and the Gallatin. Sometime, sooner or later, they'll get in at you unless Bat and his Rees do their job."

"No man talks about me that way and gets away with it!" snarled Bat.

"I am," said Miles quietly. "Keep your hand away from that pistol. You're risking the lives of these people playing at being scout."

Bat spat at Miles's feet. "He's jealous of me. I know plenty about him, Mister Carlisle. They say he's made deals with the hostiles before. Deny *that*, Flint!"

It was very quiet around the dying fire. Lorena stood up

and looked at Miles. Jonas placed his whiskey glass on the table. "What does he mean, Miles?" he said.

"I've done some trading in the past with some tribal groups for the right to hunt buffalo in their country. The Sioux and Cheyenne and the Arapahoes. They were small groups, not the whole tribe."

"You see what I mean?" crowed Bat. "He speaks their tongue. He knows their ways. He rides right through their country alone and is never bothered. How do yuh know he ain't already made a deal with them for the cattle, rifles, horses, and the *woman?*"

Miles stepped close to the scout, gripped him by the front of his fancy beaded jacket, and hit him with a short right jab that sent him staggering back against the table, scattering glasses, bottle, plates, and cutlery across the ground. Bat cursed and clawed for his pistol, but Miles closed the gap, hit him in the gut with a left hook, and followed with a right hook to the jaw that sent him smashing back against a wagon wheel. Bat rushed Miles, both arms flailing. Miles sidestepped and jumped back, tripping over a fallen chair. He went down on one knee.

Bat ripped his knife loose from its fringed beaded sheath. The dying firelight glistened from the shiny blade. Miles fell backward, driving both feet up into Bat's lean gut, raising him into the air as the blade swiped an inch away from Miles's sweating face. Miles dumped Bat on his head, then leaped to his feet to stamp a foot down on the scout's knife wrist.

Something hit Miles alongside the head. He reeled sideways and went down on one knee again. His senses reeled. Vaguely he heard Lorena screaming and the silvery chiming of spurs before he was hit again. He went down flat on his face, blood running into his dazed eyes, and rolled over to look up into the gray, expressionless face of Beck Sterret. The Texan's pistol was in his hand.

Bat had rolled up onto his feet like a cat to charge at his helpless opponent. The Colt in Beck's hand barked flatly, and the knife spun out of Bat's hand. He grunted in savage pain as he gripped his tingling hand. The echo of the shot fled through the bottoms and died away in the hills.

Miles pressed his hands to the ground to get up on his feet. His head was spinning.

"Keep yore hands away from thet sixgun," said Beck coldly.

Miles looked up at him. "When I reach for it, Sterret," he said quietly, "you'll likely damned soon know about it."

"Any time," said Sterret politely. "But not heah and now."

Jonas helped Miles to his feet. "Are you all right?" he said anxiously.

Miles nodded. He gingerly felt his lacerated scalp. "Mister Sterret buffaloes like an expert," he said dryly. "Some day I hope to pay him back with interest."

Miles picked up the whiskey bottle and drank deeply. "Thanks for the drink, Mister Carlisle," said he.

"Lorena," said Jonas. "Get bandages and medicines."

Miles shook his head. "Don't bother," he said. "Ernie can give me a hand." He did not look at Lorena. He wiped the blood from the side of his head and walked unsteadily toward the chuckwagon. Bat stood there, his eyes filled with hate, as he watched Miles walk away.

Beck Sterret looked at Jonas. "I had a feelin' somethin' like this would happen. Those two Yankees been primin' for a hassle for days. I wouldn't have the two of them together in my camp."

Jonas shrugged. "I haven't much choice, Beck."

"I ain't sayin' Flint is wrong about Batteau."

"If I leave," said Bat sullenly, "the Rees leave with me."

Neither of the two men spoke. It was as if they hadn't heard the scout speak at all.

Bat picked up his knife and inspected the blade. The slug had struck the heavy brass backing of the blade and nicked it deeply. He slid the weapon into its beaded sheath. "That was a lucky shot for Flint," he said.

Beck Sterret holstered his Colt. "That wasn't a lucky shot, Batteau," he said. "I *meant* it for the knife. But then again, it might have been a lucky shot for *you*."

Bat knew what the trail boss meant. He swaggered away from the pool of firelight.

The crying of the wolves came through the windy darkness. They seemed much closer now to the camp and to the herd.

CHAPTER TEN

The herd moved out at dawn the next day to begin the drive to Crazy Woman Creek. Beck Sterret had roused his men an hour before dawn, but there had been no sign of the Sioux and the hills had been empty and quiet except for the twittering of the birds. Beck had Old Brimstone's bell clapper loosed, and the big lead steer had started out along the ruts of the Bozeman Trail, his bell echoing from the hills until the noise of the herd's passage drowned it out.

The eyes of the drivers studied those quiet and ominous hills as the sun arose, but nothing happened. As the sun climbed higher the spirits of the Texans returned. They had two features they depended on to beat off any Sioux attack—the rolling-block rifles and the fact that most of the drivers were Texans. What more could one want? As far as the Texans were concerned, they could have eliminated the rolling-block rifles and come up with the same answer, Texans being what they say they are, and *usually* are.

Northwest, toward the distant and unseen Crazy Woman, under the clear morning sky and then under the cloud-dotted sky of early afternoon, with the bitter dust wreathing up and the ground shaking under thousands of hooves, moved the great herd of longhorns. Now and then the keenest sighted drivers thought they saw a lone horseman on the distant hills, but he would disappear before they were quite sure they had seen anything at all. The herd flowed smoothly up, over, and down the spurs of the hills, making good time toward the Crazy Woman after the noon halt. The cattle had been well watered at the Powder, and Beck Sterret had determined to drive on through the darkness to reach the Crazy Woman, a hard and waterless day's drive but well worth the effort—if the Sioux did not interfere. Maybe Beck had been right. Maybe the Sioux would not challenge the herd. They had had enough opportunities.

Late in the afternoon one of Bat's Rees, farther ahead of the herd then usual, stopped his pony between the faint ruts of the Bozeman and swung his dirty blanket back and forth over his head. Bat and the rest of the Rees, in a fan-shaped scouting front but still close enough to the herd drivers for support in case of an attack, galloped to the lone Ree. The scouts sat their horses in the middle of the road. Jonas Carlisle and Beck Sterret joined the group. Miles Flint, working along the east side of the valley, turned the bay to join them. There seemed to be something uneasy about them, something ominous.

Miles's aching head was pounding beneath the bandage when he neared the group. There was something in the middle of the road. Miles drew rein and looked at it. In the center of the road was a heap of stones from which protruded a red painted pole. To one side of the stones was a buffalo cow skull and on the other was a buffalo bull skull, both of them freshly daubed with red paint. The pole slanted toward the cow skull.

"What does it mean, Bat?" said Jonas.

Bat glanced at Miles.

"I'm asking *you*, Bat!" snapped Jonas.

Miles hooked a leg around his pommel and felt for a cigar. "War trail," he said. He lighted the cigar. "Red arrow, or buffalo skull sometimes, marks a war trail."

Beck Sterret looked up at Miles. "For us or them?"

Miles blew a smoke ring. "What difference does that make? It's a warning for us. Go no further, it means."

Beck spat tobacco at the bull's skull, splashing it liberally. "In a pig's eye," he said.

"They're just being polite. Formal," said Miles. "They didn't have to put this here."

"What does it mean?" said Jonas.

Miles leaned forward in his saddle. "It simply means that if you pass it, the Sioux will fight like buffalo bulls and we'll fight like women."

"Bullshit!" said Beck.

Miles looked at the Rees. "You'd better hogtie that bunch, Sterret, or you won't see them at dawn," he said.

"I'll take care of them Rees!" said Bat angrily.

"Best scouts and fighters on the Plains, Bat," said Miles.

Jonas looked at Miles. "What do you suggest, Miles?"

Miles looked at the empty hills and the ridge ahead of the oncoming herd. "It's your decision. There's an old saying that applies to this, and the Sioux have put the choice squarely in your trail."

"Such as?" said Beck Sterret.

"Crap or get off the pot. Put up or shut up," said Miles. "It's as simple as that."

"How far is the Crazy Woman?" said Jonas.

"Fifteen miles maybe," said Miles. "You won't make it today."

"There's no watah out heah," said the trail boss.

"You can make a dry camp or push on with thirsty, tired cattle," said Miles. "You know how easy they can be stampeded when they're like that. The Sioux can move in after dark and stampede them if you're on the trail. It wouldn't be so easy if you bunched them under guard and pushed on before dawn."

"The Sioux won't fight at night," said Bat.

"They won't have to," said Miles. "They can stampede the herd tonight without even being seen. They can do it half a dozen ways. They can set fire to the grass upwind, for one thing."

Jonas took out a cigar and bit off the end. "Maybe we should have stayed at the Powder awhile."

Beck kicked the bull skull, his spur ringing clearly. "Yuh sayin' I made a mistake, Jonas?"

"Hell no, Beck! I was all for it this morning. I was just thinking out loud."

Miles shifted in his saddle. "Have those Rees take a look-see over that ridge, Jonas," he said.

"I'm chief of scouts here!" said Bat angrily.

Miles looked at him. "Then you tell them," he said quietly.

Beck shoved back his hat and eyed the ridge. "I wonder if they'd jump us if we stayed on this side of the skulls tonight?"

Miles shrugged. "You can't ever tell," he said. Beck was beginning to get the idea. The Sioux meant exactly what they said. They never indulged in useless talk.

"All right, Bat," said Jonas. "Go on."

Bat wiped his mouth both ways. "Is that an order?" he said nervously.

"It will be full daylight for at least an hour," said Miles. "That is, if you're afraid of the dark, Bat."

Bat looked down at the skulls lying in the middle of the road. He knew as well as Miles did what it meant to pass them. *Crap or get off the pot,* Flint had said. It was a simple as that.

There was a sudden flash of crisp metal action. Bat found himself looking into the cold metal eye of the converted Navy Colt Beck Sterret carried and used so uncommonly well. *"Git,* you, and earn yore keep!" said Beck Sterret.

Bat got. He quirted his horse and set off at a gallop, followed by his Rees, like a small flock of ragged, half-starved crows, their filthy blankets hanging about their lean hips and floating behind them in the wind of their passage.

"Useless sonofabitch," said Beck. He let down the hammer of his Colt, sheathed it, then walked with softly chiming steps to his gray. "Well, Jonas, do we stay or move?"

"We stay here tonight," said Jonas.

Beck spurred toward the oncoming herd, waving his dusty hat in a circle over his head. Immediately the point drivers turned in the lead, led by Old Brimstone, so that the longhorns began a slow mill. The dust churned up and drifted off on the wind, shot through with the slanting rays of the sinking sun.

Jonas watched Bat and his Rees riding toward the ridge. "I wish I had taken your advice on them long ago, Miles," he said. "I could almost smell their green fear, amongst other things. God forgive me for making such a mistake."

"Bat puts on a prime act," said Miles. "He can fool some of the best of them."

They rode toward the dust-shrouded herd. The wind had

shifted, and the heat of the massed cattle seemed to strike at their faces.

"A dry camp," said Jonas reflectively. "I don't like this."

One of the Texans suddenly stood up in his stirrups and pointed with his rifle toward the ridge. A shot flatted off down the wind, and the echo died away in the hills.

Miles and Jonas turned in their saddles. The Rees were riding like furies down the slope, lashing their ponies at each stride. A hundred yards ahead of them was Bat Batteau, his exaggerated thrums whipping in the wind. Bat had won many a horse race on Saturday afternoons at Fort Laramie. He could have cleaned up any field of racers this day. His hat blew off and floated behind him, held by the barbequejo strap. His right arm was like a piston as it wielded the quirt on the flanks of his horse.

"Jesus God," said Jonas in an awed voice. "Look at that!"

The ridge had suddenly bloomed as the desert blooms after a spring flash storm, but there was no greenery or flowers on the ridge. It had bloomed hundreds of horsemen sitting mounts of every conceivable coloring, piebalds and paints, duns, bays, sorrels, claybanks, whites and off-whites, grays and appaloosas. War bonnets, worn only by the bravest of the brave, rippled in the dry wind. Coup sticks fluttered with colored feathers. Scalps fluttered from poles or from the fringing of leggings, while a few of the greatest warriors, the war-chiefs, had them at their horse's bits. The sun flashed from white pipe-bone breastplates, rifle barrels, pipe-axes, and other weapons.

Even the tough, battlewise Texans were hushed. They had never seen anything like this.

It was beneath the dignity of the Sioux to chase Bat Batteau and his corn Indians. These were *fighting* men, these Tetons. They sat their horses in the dying sunlight looking down impassively on the vast herd of cattle that filled the center of the valley.

"Will they attack?" said Jonas.

Miles uncased his glasses and focused them on the Sioux, scanning the long line of fierce, high-cheekboned, noble-nosed, painted faces. His glasses settled on a chief in the center of the line. His great war bonnet trailed almost to the heels of his appaloosa, and the fluffy breath feathers that trimmed the bonnet itself moved fitfully in the dry wind. Miles narrowed his eyes. He had seen that fierce visage once before, when he had ridden with Nelson Story. A touch of fear came into his mind.

"Miles?" said Jonas.

Miles lowered the glasses. "Not now. The war shields are

94

still in their covers. I think it's only a show to put the fear of God into us."

Beck Sterret had ridden up beside Jonas. "Scare who?" he said. He spat tobacco. "Let me have twenty men, Jonas. *Texans.* I'll drive them from thet ridge befoah dusk."

Miles looked at him. "By God, Sterret," he said quietly, "they might not scare you but they sure as hell scare me."

Beck spat again. He wiped his mouth. "Indians," he said. with vast contempt.

Miles cased his glasses. "That happens to be the band of Ota Kte of the Oglalas. His name means Plenty Kills, and you'd better, by God, believe it means just that."

"Will they attack tonight?" said Jonas.

Miles shook his head. "But the wolves will be in close, Jonas. None of them want to die at night, but if they think their medicine is good, they'll take a chance at a guard or in snapping up a horse. Best to get the whole corrida up an hour before dawn. It will be a lonely night for some of these younger Texas boys." Miles turned the bay and rode toward the herd.

Some of the herd had already begun to graze, and others had dropped to rest. The wagons had been corraled. The remuda was kept between the herd and the wagons. It would be hard for the young Sioux scouts not to take a crack at those horses. It was in their blood. The drivers went about their business, but they were quieter than usual, and none of them could help but steal sideways glances up at that ridge, feeling those hundreds of fierce eyes that seemed to leap the gap between ridge and herd and to strike into a man's innermost soul.

Suddenly, just as they had appeared, and almost as one, as though lifted from the ridge as a clerk would lift boxes of painted lead Indians from a toy-shop window, the warriors were gone. There was nothing to mark their passage except a lone feather blowing down the ridge toward the camp. Then the sun was gone, and the warm and windy darkness flowed into the great valley between the rolling hills and the distant Big Horns.

Miles walked through the darkness carrying the valuable snow-back pelt, still wrapped and concealed from view. He would stand guard that night as the others would, and he had stripped cantle and pommel packs from the bay. He could not carry the heavy pelt with him into action. The smell of burning buffalo chips hung over the camp mingled with the strong odor of the herd. It was quiet except for the occasional bawling of a thirsty steer, but the ominous darkness seemed to have quieted even them. Still, it wouldn't take much to get them going.

The fire within the wagon corral had been banked with earth. The drivers paced around the corral, long rifles held in the crooks of their arms, peering into the darkness. Each man had a horse saddled and tethered inside the corral. There was the faintest suggestion of moonlight in the eastern sky, but it only seemed to accentuate the thick, velvety darkness in the great valley.

A wolf howled from the ridge. A moment later another howled east of the herd. One after another the sound came until it had traveled completely around the great herd. God alone knew how many of them were out there, creeping closer and closer in the concealing darkness. The moonlight might drive them off. Bat and his frightened Rees had been sent out beyond the perimeter of the camp after each Ree had been daubed with clay moistened by the spit of Horns-in-Front, their leader. Miles placed no reliance on them. Fear might have already winged their dirty moccasins and sent them flying through the darkness toward the Powder. Still, they might be afraid to leave the protection of the trail herders.

Miles padded toward Jonas, who leaned on a rifle near the fire, an unlighted cigar in his mouth. "Indian Summer," said Miles dryly.

"It sure as hell is," said the trail herder.

Miles held out the bundled pelt. "Can you keep this in one of your wagons?"

"Sure, Miles. What is it?"

"A buffalo pelt, Jonas."

Jonas shrugged. "What's so valuable about that?"

Miles looked about. "It's an albino. On the market it's worth its weight in silver. Big medicine to an Indian, too."

"I wondered why you were so damned secretive about it. Let me have it. I'll keep it in the supply wagon." Jonas took the pelt and walked to the wagon in front of the one where he and Lorena bunked. He stowed it inside and drew the cover tightly together. "I don't want to disturb Lorena tonight so I'll sleep in this wagon." He laughed dryly. "Not that I expect much sleep tonight."

Miles walked over toward the outer line of wagons.

"Who goes dere?" came a frightened challenge.

"Miles Flint," said Miles. "How do you like standing guard, Pomp?"

"Not much. Sho' is a lot of Indians 'round heah, Mistah Flint."

Miles grinned. "Don't worry, Pomp. They will not attack tonight."

"Oh, Lawd!" said Pomp. "I hope not!"

Miles padded through the darkness. Someone was standing between two wagons. Miles reached out a hand and touched the softness of a breast. "Sorry, Lorena," he said quickly.

"You didn't know it was me," she said. She eyed him. Or did he know?

"You shouldn't be here alone," he said.

She leaned back against the wagon. "I have a gun," she said.

"Do you know how to use it?"

"Yes. Beck said to use only five of the six rounds if I had to." She looked at him again. "The sixth round is for me, if it comes to that."

"God forbid!"

She looked out in the darkness again. "I asked you long ago what they did to white women. You never told me," she said.

He looked down at her. The memory of what he had seen years ago came back to him. The torn and ravaged bodies of white women who had been "passed on the prairie," by every buck in a large war party.

"Miles?" she said. She placed a hand on his forearm.

The moonlight had touched the eastern hills. Something moved atop one of them—a wolf, or the next thing to it. It moved its head a little, and the whitish face peered back and forth exactly like that of a wolf. It raised its head. The opened mouth poured forth the melancholy, haunting cry.

"Lorena!" called Jonas. "Where are you?"

She touched Miles's face with a soft, cool hand and then was gone. Miles studied the scout atop the hill. A long shot in the bad light. Another wolf howled. Miles could see him on the next hill, squatted on a hump, his head to one side. Miles could almost see in his mind's eye the grinning face and lolling tongue of a real wolf.

The great moon swung up slowly, flooding the valley with light. It was so bright that Miles could read the lettering stamped into the metal of his Sharps barrel. The wolves had vanished from sight, but they were still up there, as their howling indicated. They likely knew they were working on the nerves of the men who stood behind the wagons, or circled the herd, softly singing. There would be no attack in that moonlight.

The herd was restless with its gigantic thirst, and now and then a sleepwalker would rise and start out from the mass of longhorns, to be turned back by a driver. There would be no sleep that night. Ernie Masland had his banked fire between the chuckwagon and the bunched remuda, and the coffeepot

97

was played heavily as the night wore on and the moon drifted slowly overhead, peering down blankly into the valley.

The moon was almost gone when Jonas came to find Miles. "Any sign of Bat and his Rees?" he said. "Cass Starr said he had seen two of them hanging around the remuda. No sign of Bat and the others, though. Maybe they pulled foot."

Miles shrugged. "Either that or they're lying plenty low," he said.

"We'll need them in close in this darkness," said Jonas.

Miles nodded. He handed his Sharps to Jonas. "I'll take a look-see," he said.

Miles stepped over a wagon tongue and walked softly along the line of wagons. He was more concerned about the guards then he was about skulking Sioux. He stopped now and then to listen. The ground was rolling, pitted here and there with great, shallow buffalo wallows. Miles shoved back his hat and rubbed his jaw. Wherever Bat was he was certainly lying low.

Miles stepped into a deeper than usual buffalo wallow. Something made him turn his head. A man stood at the lip of the wallow, looking down at Miles. If he hadn't been wearing a hat, he might have gotten a bowie blade slammed into his gut. "Thet you, Flint?" said Beck Sterret softly.

"Jesus God," said Miles in a strained tone. "You want to get yourself gutted with a Sioux knife. Get off that skyline!"

For once Beck Sterret had not heralded his coming with the chiming of his spurs. He came down the slope and faced Miles. "What are yuh doin' out heah?" he said softly.

"Looking for daisies," said Miles.

Beck raised a hand. "Damn yuh!" he snapped. "I asked yuh a question!"

"Jonas wanted me to look for Bat and his Rees."

Beck raised his head. "Out heah? They been back at the waggins for five minutes."

"Good," said Miles. "By God, I don't mind going back."

Beck did not move. "Somethin' mighty peculiar about yuh, Flint. Mebbe Bat was right at thet."

Miles stared at him. "What are you talking about?"

"I heard Bat say mor'n once he knew yuh had dealin's with Indians."

"You believe that lyin' sonofabitch?"

"No, but he made me think about it, Flint."

"This isn't the time or place for such talk, Sterret."

"Yuh make yoreself mighty big in yore boots, Flint. Comin' and goin' like yuh please. By God, yuh even acted like yuh *knowed* them Sioux was goin' to stop us today."

Miles tried to hold his temper. Sweat worked down his

sides and wet his shirt. "Get out of the way," he said thinly. "I've had enough of you this drive, Sterret."

"I thought once yuh was a squawman. I ain't so sure you ain't dealin' with these dirty redskins."

Beck Sterret was a fast man with fists, boots, or pistols, but he never saw the fist that smashed against his mouth, pasting his lips bloodily to his teeth. Before he could recover, a left smashed into his lean gut just above the big belt buckle, and as his head came down involuntarily his chin met a smashing right uppercut that snapped his head back. His breath sobbed bloodily in his throat as he went back and down under those terribly punishing blows.

Miles stepped back blowing on his skinned right knuckles. "That was for that buffaloing, you Texas sonofabitch," he said. "Get up. I've got a few more scores to settle with you, Sterret."

Beck Sterret lay there on his back, blood leaking darkly from his mouth, his eyes fixed on Miles. He could have drawn and killed Miles from where he lay but instead he got slowly to his feet. "Yuh Yankee sonofabitch," he said slowly through his smashed mouth, "I been waitin' for a chance like this." He rushed Miles, driving out a long left that Miles blocked but connecting with a right that smashed over Miles's heart, driving him back. Miles stopped Beck with a straight left jab, and the Texan closed, smashing down with booted feet on Miles's insteps as he slammed vicious and unscientific punches to Miles's face and belly. A knee drove up into Miles's crotch, and as he bent over he was hit on the jaw with a stinging right hook that sent him sprawling. He rolled over to escape the boot, grabbed the outthrust leg, and rammed himself up to his feet, upending the softly cursing trail boss so that his head hit the hard ground with stunning force. Beck rolled away from Miles's smashing feet and doubled himself on the ground until he seemed to uncoil like a tightly wound spring. His head drove up through Miles's guard and struck him on the chin, smashing his teeth together. He spat out blood and bits of powdered teeth as he drove a left against the Texan's nose, drawing blood, and then followed through with a right to the jaw that drove Beck back across the trampled grass.

They circled in the moonlight, as though the natural confines of the wallow were a fighting ring, all thought of guns and knives out of their minds as they reverted to the atavistic blood lust of savage fighting men to clash with fists, feet, and teeth.

They closed and shook each other with jolting savage punches that hurt each of them, but pain and fear were gone now. All that was left was the desire to make the other hurt and hurt again. Beck at last went down flat on his back from

99

a slugging that would have knocked out a lesser man. He lay there looking up at Miles, then got up slowly and rushed Miles almost as though nothing had happened.

Three times Miles stopped the mad rush of the Texan. Blows sounded soggily as they struck sweat-wet, bloody flesh. Then a blow hit Miles. He had not seen it coming and it lifted his feet off the ground. He smashed down on his back looking up into the bruised and bloody face of Beck Sterret. He wasn't sure he could get up again but he *had* to.

Miles opened his mouth. He slapped his hand down to his side for his Remington. Beck jumped to one side and drew just as Miles fired. Miles rolled over and over on the ground as Beck slammed a shot inches from Miles's head. "God-dammit, Beck!" yelled Miles. "Behind you! Behind you!" He fired twice from the ground.

Beck whirled, and a pipe-axe slashed the air where his head had been. He instinctively fired from the hip. The soft slug hit the Sioux buck just below the breastbone. Another buck launched himself from the rim of the wallow toward Beck, and his knife reached out like a great fang for the throat of the Texan. Miles got to his knees and fired twice. The heavy slugs drove the buck to one side.

Beck dropped to one knee and fired upward toward the skylighted warrior who stood at the lip of the wallow. He fell heavily, thrashing about in silent agony, his nerveless legs flopping about. Miles's last shot mercifully killed him.

Moccasins slapped the hard ground beyond the wallow. The powdersmoke hung heavily, being slowly rifted by the dry wind. The echo of the last shot rolled along the hills and then died away. Men yelled from the herd camp.

Miles wiped the blood from his mouth as he got up. Dazedly he flipped open the loading gate of the Remington and filled the hot cylinder with fresh cartridges while Beck swiftly reloaded his Colt. It was typical of both men.

Rifles cracked from beyond the wallow. "Got the sonofabitch!" yelled Cotton.

The bearded face of Jonas Carlisle showed over the edge of the wallow. "For the love of God," he said. "How can they come this close without being seen?"

Cass Starr and Cotton appeared beside Jonas to look down at the two battered men standing there in the wreathing powder-smoke. "Chihuahua!" said Cass. "What happened to yore face, Beck?"

Beck wiped the blood from his face. "Run into a couple of 'em at close range is all," he said.

Three pairs of eyes flicked to Miles. "Me too," said Miles.

They walked together up the wallow slope and stood beside

the three men. Three pairs of knowing eyes flicked down to abraded knuckles and then up to swollen faces, bloody noses, and puffed lips. "It musta been one helluva fracas," said Cass dryly.

"Reload that gawddam' rifle!" snapped Beck. He walked beside Miles toward the dim tilts of the wagons.

"What the hell!" said Cotton. "What was they doin' out heah anyways?"

Jonas shouldered his rifle. "The ways of the Lord are sometimes inscrutable," he said quietly.

"What the hell does thet mean?" said Cotton.

Cass spat. "Sometimes yuh ought to read a book, Cotton," he said. "Thet is, if you *can* read."

Beck stopped beside the wagons. "*Gracias*," he said.

Miles looked at him. "*Por nada*," he said.

Beck nodded. He walked off into the darkness, and although his back was ramrod straight as usual, he swayed a little in his stride. Miles gripped a wagon wheel. He wasn't feeling so steady himself.

It was quiet in the camp; the herd had settled down despite their thirst. The hilltop wolves would be gone now. In the camp of the Sioux the squaws would soon be gashing their legs with skinning knives. They would wipe the blood on the faces of the "soldiers" of the warrior societies, pleading with them to avenge the dead. Their pleas would not go unfulfilled.

CHAPTER ELEVEN

The trail camp was quietly astir in the blackness of the predawn, each man walking and working as softly as possible, although they knew they could hardly fool the Sioux. Ernie Masland had kept his fire banked all night, and the coffee was bitter as gall. But no one complained. Each driver roped his horse, stuffed hardtack into his pockets, checked his supply of cartridges, filled his big canteen from the water barrel, and went about his business.

Miles Flint finished his second cup of coffee. He touched his bruised and swollen face. Ernie Masland had studiously avoided mentioning anything about it, but everyone had a damned good idea of what had happened out there in that buffalo wallow. Fact is, both men had been on their feet, with three dead bucks lying in their own blood in the wallow. Hell's fire, it must have been a classic fight between the big Yankee and the hard-bitten Texan, and, begod, not a man to see it except a few dirty Sioux who hadn't lived long enough to talk about it.

Miles fashioned his cantle roll and swung it over the bay. He fastened it, then filled his canteen.

Chip Macklin came toward the chuckwagon. "Mistuh Carlisle heah?" he said.

"Ain't seen him, Chip," said Ernie.

"Likely out with the herd," said Miles.

Cass Starr led his claybank past the chuckwagon. "I just come back from theah," he said. "He ain't out theah, Chip."

Pomp came through the darkness. "I come for coffee for Mistuh and Mis' Carlisle, Mistuh Masland," he said.

"Help yourself, Pomp," said the cocinero. "Mister Carlisle is over there then?"

Pomp shook his head. "He didn' sleep in his Studebaker," he said.

Miles checked his Sharps and slung it. "He said he was going to sleep in one of the supply wagons," he said.

"I been callin' for him, suh," said Pomp.

Beck Sterret chimed into the group. "Wheah's them damned scouts?" he demanded.

Cass Starr shrugged. "Ain't seen them since around moonset," he said.

"Mistuh Carlisle with you, suh?" asked Pomp.

Beck shook his head. As he helped himself to a cup of coffee the faint light of the shielded lantern struck his battered face. "I ain't seen him since last night," he said.

Pomp stood there bewildered.

Miles placed a hand on the Negro's shoulder. "Take the coffee and some biscuits over there, Pomp," he said. "I'll find Mister Carlisle."

Miles walked with Chip Macklin toward the wagons. "Ain't like him," said Chip. "Mis' Carlisle been askin' for him."

Miles saw Lorena standing beside her wagon, dressed in her Confederate gray riding habit, her mare tethered to the wheel beside her. Miles walked to the supply wagon where Jonas had stowed the buffalo pelt. Chip Macklin had already harnessed the mules to it.

"Jonas?" said Miles.

There was no answer. Miles parted the wagon cover. "Jonas?" he said. He waited a moment and then thrust in a hand. Something sliced into the side of it. He snatched back his hand and

102

thrust it into his mouth. "Damn it! He stuck me with a knife!" he said.

"Mister Carlisle?" said Chip. "That ain't likely, Miles."

Chip pulled aside the cover and snapped a match on his thumbnail. "Jesus God!" he said. He quickly dropped the cover and looked back at Lorena Carlisle.

"What is it, man?" said Miles.

"Look for yourself," said the wagon driver. "But don't let her see!"

Miles pulled back the cover and lighted a match. In the wavering light he saw Jonas Carlisle lying face downward on a pile of sacks. Something alien protruded from the trail driver's back. It was a yellowish-white, bone-handled knife, and it was buried almost to the hilt in Jonas Carlisle's body. It was that which had cut Miles. He dropped the cover and looked quickly toward Lorena.

Somewhere in the darkness a driver had loosed Old Brimstone's bell clapper. It sounded clearly through the darkness. The herd was grunting to its feet.

Lorena walked toward Miles and Chip. Spurs chimed behind her, and Beck Sterret, with that uncanny sixth sense of his, showed up where the trouble was. "What is it, Miles?" said Lorena.

Miles looked away. He gripped the side of the wagon

"Miles?" she said.

"Yuh got to tell her, Miles," said Chip out of the side of his mouth.

"Don't look in the wagon," said Miles to Lorena.

She looked uncertainly at him. "He's in theah, isn't he?"

Miles nodded.

"He's hurt?" she said quietly.

Miles looked at Beck Sterret. The Texan nodded. Miles took the young woman by the shoulders. "Jonas is dead," he said softly.

She buried her head against his chest, and her body shook. Miles looked over her head at Beck. "God knows how they got in this close."

Beck looked at the woman, and his meaning was clear. *Thank God they hadn't gotten to her.*

Lorena raised her head. She fought to compose herself. "What shall we do now?" she said.

Beck took off his hat. "It's yore herd now, ma'am," he said simply. "I got to take yore orders, ma'am."

She raised her head again and looked at the tough trail boss, at homely Chip Macklin, at little Pomp, and then at Miles Flint. "The way to the Gallatin is north," she said.

Beck smiled swiftly, then turned on his heel. He chimed

off into the darkness to get the herd moving toward the crossing of the Crazy Woman.

Lorena stepped back from Miles. "There's no time to bury him properly heah," she said. A tear rolled down her cheek. "We'll take my husband's body to the Crazy Woman and bury him theah, gentlemen." She turned and walked to her mare.

Miles nodded to Chip. The driver tied the cover shut and walked to the front of the wagon. As the first faint touch of false dawn made itself known in the eastern sky the wagons rolled on behind the slowly moving herd.

Miles looked at Lorena. She touched her mare lightly with her quirt and rode on after the wagons. This day would be one of pure hell for her.

Miles walked to his bay and untethered it. He swung up into the saddle and rode toward the front of the herd. Beck Sterret turned in his saddle. "God help her," he said.

Miles nodded. "Where are Bat and his Rees?"

"Pulled foot," said the trail boss.

"I thought so," said Miles.

"We'll have to go on without them, Flint."

Miles shoved back his hat and felt for a cigar. He lighted it. "I'll try to keep one ridge ahead of you, Sterret," he said. "About all I can do is warn you. You'll likely have no more than a few minutes to get ready, but it might mean the difference between life and death." He touched the bay with his heels and galloped off into the lonely darkness ahead of the herd.

Cass Starr shifted his chew and spat. "Theah goes a man, Beck," he said.

Beck Sterret did not answer. He touched his gray with his spurs and rode down the side of the herd, his hard gray eyes, one of them well puffed, taking in everything.

The wind shifted with the coming of the false dawn. Each shadow on the rolling ground seemed to hold hidden menace to the drivers, and they gripped their Remingtons just a little tighter.

Miles Flint felt the cool wind against his bruised face. The ridge was a dim line against the northern horizon like a barrier between the herd and the Sioux. To Miles it was more of a psychological barrier than the red-daubed buffalo skulls had been. An uneasy feeling came to rest on his shoulders. He passed beyond the sound of the herd and seemed to move into a little world of his own as he rode up the slope of the ridge. Far behind him the herd moved north. Old Brimstone was squarely in the middle of the road, as was his custom. His hooves struck the pile of stones, snapped the red-painted pole, and scattered the red-painted skulls. The grinding hooves of the herd smashed the skulls into powder. It was too late to go back now.

Miles loosed the Spencer carbine in its sheath. Jonas had issued him one from his supply of extra weapons. Miles preferred the stubby carbine to the longer-ranged single-shot Remingtons. The repeater carried seven rounds of bottle-necked .56/50 caliber cartridges in the magazine and one more in the chamber, and he had three brass reloading tubes containing seven cartridges each with which he could refill the butt magazine in jig time. With the repeating carbine and his Remington pistol he could give a good account of himself at short range, but it would hardly be adequate to stop a concerted charge of Cheyenne Dog Soldiers or Sioux Kit Foxes. The Sharps could hold off an attack at the longer ranges. If he was wounded or unhorsed at the outset of a fight, he wouldn't stand a chance.

He breasted the crest of the ridge. There was no time to scout by sight, sound, or smell. He'd have to look right now and keep pushing on if there was no sign of the hostiles. The northern slope was empty of life as far as he could see. The grass was moving dimly in the faint light as the wind swept it. There was no odor of pony droppings or of burning buffalo chips.

As the light grew brighter he could see much farther, and by the time he reached the next ridge he could see that the country, so far at least, was empty of the Sioux. He eased the bay. He might need all of his reserve strength before too long. An eerie loneliness came over him. The old gnawing fear of the plainsman came to roost in his mind. What was beyond those empty-looking hills?

He looked back to see Old Brimstone top the last ridge, followed by the other lead steers and guided by the two point riders. Suddenly the rising sun flashed from the many horns of the cattle. Miles lighted a cigar. The Sioux were experts in hitting you where and when you least expected it. There were no finer light cavalry in the world, and it was a gigantic error to think that they wouldn't or couldn't fight under their own type of discipline.

Hour after hour passed slowly by, with the trail dust rising into the bright sunlight. Beck Sterret would allow no noon halt. There would be no water before the Crazy Woman. The trail drivers changed mounts practically on the move and raced back to their posts. But there was still no sign of the Sioux—not even a pile of droppings from one of their ponies.

Miles found it hard to believe when at last he reined in the bay and looked far down the long grassy slope toward the crossing of the Crazy Woman. The willows and cottonwoods bordering the stream swayed in the dry wind. Heat waves shimmered up from the ground, and the late-afternoon sun sparkled from the rippling waters. Miles lighted a cigar. "Beats the hell outta me," he said thoughtfully.

Maybe the Oglalas thought their medicine had failed because of the deaths of their scouts the night before. Those who had died could not cross the Great Shadow Waters because they had been killed at night. It wouldn't be fear of the white men, but rather fear of their medicine that might be holding them back.

Miles heard, faintly at first, the bawling of the cattle and the braying of the mules as the shifting wind brought the tantalizing scent of the fresh water to them. He turned to look back at them. Old Brimstone rose over a ridge and strode steadily down the center of the faint track of the Bozeman. Beck Sterret rode close beside him, his right hand resting lightly on Old Brimstone's left horn tip. Two of a kind, thought Miles; set them to a job and they'll do it, come hell or high water.

The herd came closer and closer. The wagons jounced and bounced over the rougher ground. Lashes popped over the long, dusty ears of the mules. Dust swirled thickly down the slopes. The way was clear to the Crazy Woman at least; Miles had done the job that should have been done by Bat Batteau and his Rees. He stood up in his stirrups. He had been lucky at that, for one man could hardly cover all the approaches to the Crazy Woman. He sat down and kneed the bay toward the closest hills. From the top of one of them he could see the country northeasterly along the valley of the Crazy Woman. He urged the tired bay up the slope.

Somewhere behind him, beyond the Bozeman Trail, in the cut-up ground thickly strewn with trees, a sound arose like grease popping in a gigantic skillet. Miles snapped his head around. A sickle of feathered horsemen seemed to rise out of the ground itself, to the west of the herd *and almost behind it*. They screamed and fired, while some of them flapped blankets to stampede the tired, thirsty longhorns. Miles hurled his cigar aside and launched the bay down the slope. He had done his part by seeing that the way *ahead* of the herd was clear. But the Sioux, knowing there was only one scout ahead of the herd, had played it smart by *tailing* the herd, because Bat Batteau and his Rees had not been there as they should have been to cut for Sioux sign and warn the trail drivers.

Damn Beck Sterret! The thought raged through Miles's mind as he raced toward the herd. The Texan should have flung out some of his men to watch the vulnerable flanks of the herd and to take up some of the shock of that swiftly approaching charge. Even a Texan should have known enough to do that! Where the hell had *he* gone to war!

The remuda stampeded, smashing into the line of fast-moving wagons. Rifles began to flash and crack from the wagons and from the flanks of the herd. Here and there in the swirling dust blossomed orange-red bursts of gunfire.

Three horses, driven by two shrieking bucks, broke from the remuda and raced along the slope. Another buck rode right into the center of the remuda and transferred himself from his paint pony to the back of a rearing sorrel, clinging like a monkey on a stick, guiding the sorrel through the press, followed by the paint pony. Only a leg and an arm showed as target for the cursing Texans.

A knot of pounding steers struck the side of the chuckwagon just as it hit the ruts and bounced up on two wheels. The weight of the steers dumped it over, wheels spinning, and the mules began to kick each other to death in the tangle of harness. A supply wagon smashed into the dumped chuckwagon, and the driver flew from the seat, arms outspread, just as a buck drove in close and fired a double-barreled shotgun full into his face. He was dead before he hit the ground.

Miles reined in the bay and fired swiftly, three times, slamming the lever down and up and firing the instant the breech was closed. A warrior's horse went down. A buck died with a slug in his screaming mouth. A third buck badly wounded bounced on the hard ground, dragged by his frightened pony.

Beck Sterret and Cass Starr drove into a knot of Sioux, firing six-shooters from both hands, and left half a dozen Sioux dead or writhing on the dusty ground.

A dozen horses had been driven off along with at least fifty longhorns, but the herd was on its way to the waters of the Crazy Woman and nothing could stop them, and to hell with the Texans, the Sioux, and everything else.

Miles emptied the smoking Spencer, flipped open the loading gate in the butt plate, and poured in seven fresh rounds in a matter of seconds. He kneed the lathered bay toward the herd, slamming shot after shot into the speeding feathered horsemen who appeared and disappeared in the thick swirling cloud of dust.

The Sioux were breaking for the ridge, driving the captured longhorns and horses ahead of them. Here and there other warriors held onto the flanks of the herd and snapped shots at the dusty Texans. Beck Sterret led a quartet of drivers toward the captured animals. Miles raced toward them. He drove his bay close beside the trail boss. "For God's sake, don't follow them over that ridge. Sterret! They're waiting for you! They'll cut you to pieces! Let them have those longhorns!"

107

Beck stared at Miles through a mask of dust. For a moment there was no recognition, but then sanity came to him. "All right, boys," he said. "Back to the herd!"

"Dammit, Beck!" yelled George Livesey. "We can git 'em back!"

"No!" yelled the trail boss. "Flint is right! We'd nevah git back! Back to the herd! That's yore job now!"

Already Old Brimstone had reached the Crazy Woman and the bellowing cattle were flowing into the creek after him, filling the shallow waters of the crossing from bank to bank, spreading up and down stream. No one, not Old Brimstone or Beck Sterret or even a passel of shrieking Sioux, could make them move from that water.

Miles reloaded the hot, smoking Spencer. Above the uproar of the bawling steers and ripple of gunfire he heard a scream that somehow sounded different from the voices of the Sioux. The whole herd now filled the Crazy Woman, bank to bank up and down the stream as far as the eye could see. The Texans were bunched together, firing steadily at the last few bucks who were racing uphill to where the longhorns and captured horses had vanished, leaving a pall of bitter dust to mark their passing.

Miles stopped beside the dumped chuckwagon. Ernie Masland was nursing a broken arm. Cass Starr and several drivers threw loops over the wagon wheels and pulled the wagon back upright. Pots and pans flew as the wagon smashed down. The Texans untangled the harness, shot two of the broken-legged mules, then one of them drove the wagon down to the creek.

Miles shoved back his hat and wiped the sweat from his face. It had been cheap enough at half the price. Here and there in the settling dust lay dead warriors. Two Texans lay dead, as well as one of the drivers of a supply wagon.

All of the wagons were moved to the shelter of the willows and cottonwoods of the creek bottom. Beck Sterret placed a line of mounted drivers between the herd and the open ground. Others gathered near the wagons. Miles rode slowly down the slope toward them. There would be more than one burial beside the Crazy Woman that evening.

Beck Sterret looked up at Miles. "Wheah's Mis' Carlisle, Flint?" he said in a strained voice.

Miles stared at him. He looked at other taut, dusty faces. He looked back toward the scattered bodies on the open ground.

"She ain't out theah, Flint," said Cotton.

"She ain't around heah either," said Chip Macklin.

Then something came back to Miles. That scream he had heard. He turned in his saddle and looked up the ridge to the hill where the captured horses and longhorns had been

108

driven, still marked by a drifting wraith of thin dust shot through with the last rays of the sinking sun.

"My God! No!" said Cass Starr.

Miles touched the bay with his heels and rode up the slope alongside the ruts of the Bozeman. Half a mile from the creek he saw the sun glinting from something. It was a silver-mounted six-shooter, chased and engraved. He slid from his saddle and picked it up. The initials L.A.C. had been engraved on each side of the butt frame. "Lorena Alice Carlisle," he said aloud. He opened the loading gate. Five cartridges had been expended. The last one was still in the chamber. *"Beck said to use only five of the six rounds if I had to,"* she had said. *"The sixth round is for me, if it comes to that."*

Miles swung up onto the bay and rode toward the creek. The wind had shifted, driving the yellowish dust across the Crazy Woman and over the backs of the longhorns. *"I asked you long ago what they did to white women,"* she had also said. *"You never told me."*

CHAPTER TWELVE

They forted up in the bottoms, corraling the wagons, keeping the longhorns close herded, doubling the number of night herders. Now and then a shot cracked out as something moved in the brush beyond the herd. It wouldn't be easy to stampede the longhorns from the water and the thick grass of the bottoms, and the Sioux had learned respect for the rolling-block Remingtons and the accuracy of the men who used them.

Spades rang against the ground as a common grave was dug for the dead. A shielded bull's-eye lantern showed just enough light to place the blanket-wrapped forms into the grave. Ernie Masland brought the worn Bible from the chuckwagon. Those drivers who could be spared gathered in the little clearing. The service was solemn but swift. There was little time now for the dead. It was the living that mattered.

Beck Sterret walked beside Miles Flint back to the chuckwagon. "We owe it to Jonas and ouahselves to git Mis' Carlisle back, Flint," he said.

Miles shook his head. "Impossible," he said firmly.

"We can leave a few men with the herd. Them Sioux won't

likely be able to stampede the herd from heah. Yuh say they won't fight at night. *Bueno!* We kin fight at night."

"You wouldn't get two miles from here, Sterret, and they'd have you cut off. You know that as well as I do."

The trail boss smashed a fist into his other palm. "Jesus, oh, Jesus," he said. "It was my fault! I was so damn' busy watchin' them beeves I forgot about her."

"We were all busy," said Miles. Thoughts about rescuing Lorena raced through his mind, but none of them made any sense. She was young and pretty. Some honored buck might want her for a squaw, and in that case she might be unharmed by the others, but if she was not wanted. . . . Miles knew one thing for sure; no white man could leave the valley of the Crazy Woman and come back alive. A regiment of cavalry couldn't do it. Five miles from Fort Phil Kearny, shortly after the war, three officers and seventy-nine men had chased a small party of Sioux into the hills, and not a man of them had come back. They had hardly been a match for the estimated two thousand Sioux and Cheyenne who had trapped them. That had been thirty miles north of the crossing of the Crazy Woman.

"Gawd's sake!" burst out the trail boss. "We can't stand here doin' nothin'!"

Miles fashioned a cigarette. He lighted it. "There's one long chance," he said.

"Name it!"

Miles walked to the supply wagon where Jonas Carlisle had died. He rooted around in it feeling for the wrapped albino pelt. He couldn't find it. He lighted match after match and looked thoroughly. The pelt just wasn't in there. He dropped from the tailgate, and as he did so something rang on the ground. Miles picked up the bone-handled knife that had killed Jonas.

"He'p, yuh?" said Chip Macklin.

"There was a wrapped buffalo pelt in here, Chip," said Miles, hefting the knife. "You take it out?"

"Haven't touched a thing, Miles. Mebbe it fell out."

Miles nodded. "Maybe."

Pomp came slowly through the darkness. "You goin' after Mis' Carlisle, Mistuh Flint?" he said miserably.

"We'll do the best we can, Pomp."

"I'll go along too, suh," said the little Negro.

Miles knew he was scared to death of the Sioux, but he knew Pomp meant it.

The light from the shielded lantern touched the knife Miles had in his hand. Pomp eyed it. "Mistuh Batteau done forgot his knife when he left," he said. "Mistuh Batteau set a heap of store

110

by that knife. He tole me he made it outta the arm bones of the Indian he kill hand-to-hand. Bull-ovah-the-Mount'in, somethin' lak that."

"Bull-over-the-Hill," said Miles. He looked down at the knife and then up at Chip Macklin. "Jesus Christ!" he said.

Chip nodded. "Yeh. No wonder the killer got past the guards," he said quietly. "He was in camp all the time."

Things fitted together in Miles's mind. The disappearance of Bat and his Rees the same night Jonas had been murdered. The disappearance of the valuable snow-back buffalo pelt.

A rifle cracked amongst the willows. "Kill the sonofabitch!" yelled a Texan.

There was a thrashing noise, and a dark figure splashed into the stream. "God's sake, don't shoot ol' Guts!" screamed the odd-sounding voice.

"Lemme git a shot at him, Cotton!" yelled Ben Horton.

Miles ran to the stream edge. "Don't shoot that man!" he yelled. "Hold your fire!"

The dark figure crawled out of the stream, shaking with fright. Miles wrinkled his nose at the stench of the man and dragged him toward the shielded bull's-eye lantern. A fantastic sight met the eyes of the onlookers. A battered, greasy stovepipe hat, topped by a bedraggled feather sat crookedly atop the dark, braided hair of the man. The dirty, grayish braids were wrapped with raccoon skin. He wore a ragged military vest over his bare upper body. A threadbare blanket hung like a kilt about his bowed legs. On his feet were moccasins from which depended a rusty pair of huge Mexican spurs. Miles plucked a knife from its sheath and dropped it on the ground. He removed a huge double-barreled, percussion-lock pistol from the man's belt.

The captive looked about wildly at the hard faces of the men who surrounded him. He was like a frightened captive animal, more animal than human.

"Hello, Guts," said Miles. "You're out late tonight."

"Befo' God, Misser Flint," he blurted. A sob broke his voice. "I done nothin'! I was just lookin' for dried meat and gravy biscuit! I ain't with them Oglalas! I just Guts! Good ol' Guts, thass all!"

"Yeh," said Miles dryly. "Good ol' Guts, thass all!" He pulled the breed to his feet, wincing at the sour stench of the man. "What the hell are you doing around here?"

"They leave ol' Guts alone?" said the breed. He looked fearfully over his shoulder. "They kill ol' Guts' mule."

Miles gripped him by the vest front. "Tell me the truth, you breed bastard," he said thinly. "What are you doing here?"

"I come to see Batteau."

"Why Batteau?" said Miles.

"Batteau owe me money."

"For what?" said Miles.

The loose dirty face of the breed seemed to shift in and out of focus. "He tells Guts when is best time for attack," he said. He grinned widely. "Guts tell Lakota."

Spurs chimed. "Let me at him," said Beck Sterret.

"Wait," said Miles. "This poor bastard doesn't know the difference between right and wrong. He'll help you as well as hinder you for a price. We need information right now. He might just have it."

Guts smiled. He was on familiar ground now. "Sure, sure," he said quickly. "Guts tell. Guts know everything. Guts get money, horse, gun, food, maybe wo-haw?"

"Guts will get his filthy guts torn out," said Beck.

Miles pushed Guts back against a wagon. "You mean Batteau sent you on ahead to tell the Lakotas about this trail drive?"

"Thass Guts' business," said the breed.

Miles pushed a little, and the breed's head struck the side of the wagon. His plug hat hung rakishly over one bloodshot eye. He knew better than to try to force information out of the breed, for Guts had ethics of his own; he simply had to be paid, one way or another, for what he knew.

"Tell me about Batteau, Guts," said Miles. He shook the breed a little.

"Guts get paid?"

"Guts get paid," said Miles.

Guts grinned. "Bat say he take away Rees at right time. Rees no good. Rees dirty. Rees Corn Indians. Not like ol' Guts. Ol' Guts Sans Arc. Guts talk to Lakota. Lakota know when Rees leave. Come in behind. Ha! Ha! Ol' Miles Flint, he in front with gun that shoot today, kill tomorrow. Ha! Ha!"

Miles shoved Guts's head back against the wagon. "Ha! Ha!" he mimicked. "Where's Batteau now?"

"Ol' Bat, he not here?" said the breed in surprise.

"You dumb bastard," said Miles thinly. "You think he'd come back here after he pulled foot and let us walk into the Lakotas?"

Guts waggled his head. "He say he *might* be here. If not, he say *you* pay me off. He make deal with ol' Miles Flint. Miles Flint, he pay off Guts."

Beck Sterret moved. "So?" he said.

Miles looked back at him. "Don't be a damned fool, Sterret," he said. "Don't you get Bat's game? He sends this fool here to get paid off. Sure, Guts would have been paid off— with a slug in his head!"

Guts waggled his head. "Bat say trail boss owe him money for scouting. Ol' Guts collect and keep. Good deal, hey?"

Miles released the breed. "You're lucky you're not dead now," he said.

"You not pay ol' Guts?" said the breed incredulously.

There was no use in explaining it to the breed. "Where is Batteau?" said Miles.

The bloodshot eyes shifted. Guts picked at his broken nose and feigned indifference. He scuffed his moccasins in the dirt and cleared his throat.

"A good horse to replace your mules," said Miles.

Guts twisted a braid, looked up at the sky, examined a button on his vest.

"What more do you want?" said Miles.

Guts grinned. "Gun that loads today, shoots all week," he said in a wild rush of words. His eyes gleamed.

"It's yours," said Miles. "With two boxes of cartridges."

Guts bobbed his head delightedly.

"Why did Bat pull foot so suddenly?" said Miles.

Guts looked about. "Bat got big medicine," he said in an awed voice.

Miles gripped him by his greasy vest. "Such as a snow-back buffalo pelt?"

Guts nodded. "Big medicine! Big! Big! Bat want to trade pelt to Lakota. Afraid to go near camp. Bat tell Guts to go to Lakotas. Guts no afraid of Lakotas. Bat want Guts to go to camp of Lakotas and make deal for Bat. Then Guts to come here for pay. Bat smart. Guts smarter. Guts come here to get paid first, *then* go to camp of Ota Kte. Guts no fool, hey?"

"Were you in the camp of the Lakotas?"

"Long time ago. Guts watch fight today. See Lakotas run off spotted buffalo and horses."

"Did you see a white woman with them?"

Every eye was on the breed. Again the feigned indifference; the detached, pensive air.

"A good hunting knife," said Miles.

Guts rubbed his greasy face.

"What is it you want?" said Miles.

Guts went into an act as though winding something, then holding it up to his ear in great delight.

"A watch?" said Miles. "It's yours."

"Woman with Lakotas. White woman. Clothes torn. Guts see bare white tits. Ha! Ha! Woman's face wet. Cry allatime."

"She's safe?"

Guts rolled eyes upward. "Mebbe, Mebbe not. Not know. Lakotas sometimes crazy with white squaws. Sometimes kill. Sometimes screw. Sometimes marry."

113

"You can find Batteau?"

"Mebbe."

Miles shook his head. "Sack of flour. Sack of beans. Bag of coffee."

"Guts show you."

"Is it far?"

"Not far."

Miles walked to Beck Sterret. Half a dozen drivers stood with the big trail boss. "With that snow-back pelt I might be able to dicker with the Sioux," said Miles in a low voice.

"You've got to git it away from Bat and his Rees first," said Beck Sterret. "How many men do you want?"

Miles held up two fingers.

Beck turned. "Cotton?"

"Yuh know it, Boss," said the young Texan.

"Who else?" said Miles.

Beck turned. "Are you joshin'?" he said. "I want to see Bat and his Rees once more. Thet should be enough."

The valley was shrouded in premoon darkness when the four horsemen rode on hoof-muffled horses into the dark, forbidding hills bordering the Crazy Woman.

It was Guts who picked up the faint odor of burning buffalo chips as the moon hung low atop the Big Horns. Guts stopped his horse at the mouth of a tree-filled ravine. He bobbed his head up and down. His meaning was plain enough.

Miles leaned close to the breed. "How many?" he whispered.

"Batteau and four Rees," said Guts.

Miles swung down and tethered his bay to a tree. "No shooting," he said quietly.

"We got knives, ain't we?" said Beck.

Miles nodded. "Bat is mine," he said.

"We owe yuh thet," said Cotton.

"Watch the horses," said Miles to Guts.

Beck Sterret fingered his knife. "Mebbe he'll pull out," he said.

Miles shook his head. "Looney as he is, once he makes a deal he keeps it. That's more than you can say for a helluva lot of white men."

Miles let his hat drop to the back of his neck. The two Texans did the same, then removed their spurs. Miles led the way down into the darkness of the ravine. He went bellyflat as he neared a clearing, faintly lighted by the dying moon. The smell of burning chips was stronger, mingled with the acrid odor of horse droppings. The wind blew a little stronger, lifting the ashes from atop the fire and revealing the winking red eyes of low flame. There were four blanketed forms lying with their feet toward the fire. Beyond them, seated against

114

a tree, was another blanket-wrapped form with a rifle lying across his lap. Miles watched him for a time. He did not move. Likely the guard was asleep or at least dozing.

Miles tested the honed edge of his heavy bowie knife. He looked at the two hardfaced Texans, pointed to the guard, then to himself. They nodded. Miles worked his way bellyflat through the tangle of brush and rustling fallen leaves. A horse whinnied softly upwind. Miles worked his way behind the guard. Beyond the fire and the sleepers he saw two shadowy forms. Miles slid an arm around the tree and the guard's throat and pinned the guard back against the tree. He struggled a little. Miles put on more pressure. The moccasined heels of the Ree beat a soft tattoo on the leaf-covered ground and then stopped. Miles eased the dead Ree to the ground and stood up. He motioned toward the sleeping forms.

The two Texans came in on catfeet. A knife rose and fell. A Ree gasped once. Another thrust of a knife and a Ree grunted, raised his head, then let it fall back again with a thud. The third Ree sat up and opened his mouth to yell. Beck hit him from the back at the same time Cotton caught him gut low.

The last sleeper awoke. He stared at Beck and Cotton, blood-dripping knives in their hands. It was Bat Batteau. He leaped to his feet from the tangle of blankets and bolted for the horses. Miles hurdled a log and ran lightly on moccasined feet after Bat. Bat turned once and saw that grim hawk's face behind him. He opened his mouth to scream in terror just as the bowie left Miles's hand in an overhand whip. The heavy brass-backed blade sank deeply in between Bat's shoulderblades. He was still running when death claimed him and brought him crashing to earth.

Miles walked on catfeet to the scout. He withdrew the bowie and kicked the scout over on his back. He wiped the blade clean on the exaggerated thrums.

"Yuh throw a *cuchillo* like a greaser," said Cotton.

"Make sure of them." said Miles, jerking his head toward the Rees.

"We know ouah business," said Beck.

Miles kicked aside Bat's blankets. The wrapped snow-back pelt had been Bat's last pillow on earth. Miles cut the thrums to make sure it was the pelt. He tied it together and stood up.

"What now, Flint?" said Beck.

Miles shrugged. "I'll try to make a dicker with Ota Kte," he said.

"With thet hide?" said Cotton. "Yore loco."

Miles looked at him. "You got any better ideas?"

There was no answer. Miles whistled softly three times.

Guts led up the four horses. Miles tied the pelt to his cantle roll and mounted the bay. "Take the other horses back with you, Sterret. The remuda could use a few replacements. If I'm not back with Mrs. Carlisle in forty-eight hours, you can use your own judgment with the herd. Go back to the Platte or on to the Gallatin. You can let Ernie Masland have my Sharps."

Cotton looked at the dead men. "What about this carrion heah?" he said.

"Let the ravens gather," said Miles. "Come on, Guts." The two of them rode from the darkening ravine.

Beck spat tobacco juice. "I think I know now wheah I seen him befo'," he said quietly as he wiped the juice from his mouth.

Cotton rolled a cigarette. "Yeh? Wheah, Beck?"

"Durin' the wah. At Gettysburg. He was lookin' ovah the sights of one of them damned hairsplittin' Sharps at us boys of the Fifth Texas. Yeh. It was him, all right."

Cotton snapped a match on his thumbnail and lighted the cigarette. "Yuh think he'll come back, Beck?"

Beck swung up onto his gray. He rested his hands on the pommel and looked down at his companion. "I ain't bettin' on it," he said.

"Me neither."

They rode from the ravine leading the extra horses. The wind flared up the fire. The yellow light reflected from the staring eyes of the dead. Somewhere in the hills a wolf howled.

CHAPTER THIRTEEN

The late afternoon sun hung over the Big Horns, the rays slanting down into the timbered valley through which a clear stream wandered in serpentine fashion. Guts drew rein and turned in his saddle. He pointed up the valley. There was a faint wraith of smoke drifting upward in the almost windless air.

"How far?" said Miles.

"T'ree miles mebbe, mebbe little more." Guts grinned. "If Lakota let you get that far."

"Never mind about that," said Miles. He turned in his saddle and looked back the way they had come. The sun's rays slanted through the timber. There wasn't a sign of life. For all Miles knew they might have been seen long ago.

"This back way," said Guts. "Main way farther north. Lakota there. Many. Many. Guts take long way around. Guts no want to see Lakota now."

Miles dismounted. He unbuckled the carbine sheath and handed it and the Spencer to Guts. He unbuckled his gunbelt, heavy with sheathed Remington and bowie knife, and draped it over the withers of Guts's horse. "These are yours. The horse you ride is yours. Go back to the camp and get the rest of the things we agreed upon. Fair enough?"

Guts looked up the valley with feigned indifference.

"Damn you!" said Miles. He removed his gold repeater watch from inside his jacket and handed it to Guts. "My father gave me that watch when I went to war."

Guts grinned. "Nice father," he said. "Never knew mine."

"You dirty bastard," said Miles under his breath as he mounted the bay.

Guts nodded. "Guts dirty bastard. Guts too smart to go into Lakota camp." He watched Miles ride down the slope toward the stream. *"H'gun, h'gun,"* said Guts. It was the Sioux courage word.

Miles splashed across the shallow stream and looked back. Guts had vanished. Miles pressed a hand down on the rolled snow-back pelt and kneed the bay to ride upstream. It was quiet except for the twittering of the birds, and even that sound died away as he advanced. The wind arose a little and brought with it the faint odor of horse droppings. He cleared the timber and rode into a meadowland area. His heart failed a little as he looked to the far side of the meadow and saw the mass of the horse herd. It was one big helluva herd, much bigger than he had expected. "This is a good day to die," he said. "Have courage."

A young horse guard saw him first. He rode a little closer, peered at Miles, then raised a long-barreled rifle. Miles dropped the reins and guided the bay with his knees. He raised both hands, palms outward, and rode slowly toward the guard. The guard raised his voice in a shrill, penetrating cry that echoed back from the valley sides.

Miles reined in the bay and waited. There would be no going back if he waited just a few minutes longer. The hair prickled on the back of his neck. He heard the raucous cries of the blackbirds as they fluttered over the ponies, snapping up the grasshoppers stirred up by the grazing herd. The wind

117

shifted a little and swayed the trees. Leaves fell in a pale-yellow shower, some of them swirling along on the surface of the stream.

He seemed to feel something behind him. He turned slowly in his saddle. Four bucks sat their horses fifty yards from him, rifles or carbines across their thighs, the wind swaying the feathers they were wearing. Miles took out a cigar and lighted it, trying to keep his hands from shaking. The way of retreat was closed now. He could do nothing but go forward, and God have mercy on Miles Flint, sinner.

The young horse guard came trotting toward Miles, followed by an older warrior. The two of them halted their horses and looked at Miles. He again made the sign of peace. No expression crossed their faces. They could see that he was alone and unarmed. They had nothing to lose. Their curiosity was probably getting the better of them.

The day was late. Herders appeared around the flanks of the herd and began to drive them toward the unseen village for the night. Miles blew a smoke ring and thrust a finger through it. Still no movement from the two watching bucks. Then something touched Miles in the small of the back. He didn't have to look to know that it was a rifle muzzle. The older buck jerked his head toward the upper part of the valley. Miles touched the bay with his heels and rode in that direction, not looking back into the four grim faces behind him.

He could see the smoke rising from the village before he saw it, and then the harsh barking of many dogs came to him. His two guides rode up and over a slope. As he reached the crest he saw the village spread out before him in concentric rings, with the opening facing the east as it always did. In the center of the village he could see the big council tepee and a smaller red-painted medicine tepee just beyond it. It was a big village, a very big village. This was no temporary hunting camp or the village of a small band. This was a semi-permanent camp.

They knew he was coming. Squaws stood in front of their lodges looking toward the strange *Wasicun* who rode toward them. The warriors had grouped themselves nearer the center of the village, on the bare, pounded ground before the council lodge and the medicine tepee. They almost filled the cleared area. Miles reached the first ring of lodges, passing many racks upon which hung blackened strips of drying buffalo meat, hundreds and hundreds of pounds of it. It would be a good winter for the village of Ota Kte.

Although the village looked as though each lodge had been set up at whim, Miles knew that each lodge always had a

118

certain place in the order and that this order was never broken. It was the ancient custom. Thus each village circle had a place for each band within it, and each band had a certain place for each lodge of that particular band so that every member of the village had a specific "address." Beside each lodge was tethered the night horse of the owner so that he need never be caught by surprise without a mount. Before each lodge was a tripod from which hung the owner's personal medicine bundle, a case containing a war bonnet, if he rated one, and often some of his weapons and his cased war shield. On some of the lodges pictographs depicted the deeds of the owner, although some warriors preferred these on a robe rather than on the lodge skins.

He saw the impassive faces of the squaws and their strong brown hands. If he was killed at once, it would be the work of a brave. If he was saved for the work of the squaws, he might live for a long time before they let him die. An icy feeling came into his guts. One of their favorite tricks was to saw off a living man's genitals with a dull-edged knife. He could almost read their thoughts as he rode past them. Would he be so brave pegged out like a drying hide while the squaws worked on him? *Hoh?*

He neared the massed warriors. Many of them had their faces painted red for luck, but here and there a black-painted face stood out, indicating that the warrior had recently killed an enemy . . . perhaps some of the men who had ridden with the trail herd. He looked beyond the massed warriors to see a tall, broad-shouldered warrior standing in front of the council lodge. He was over six feet in height, and Miles had no difficulty in recognizing him. It was Ota Kte, the Oglala war-chief with at least fifty coups, and entitled to wear on his war bonnet the bison horns that signified his position as one of the bravest of the brave.

The warriors parted to leave a narrow path for Miles to approach the chief, but he knew better than to do this mounted. He swung down from the bay, inches away from the nearest warriors, trying to keep his eyes away from their hands gripping sheathed scalping knives. He casually ground out the cigar. He had never felt so utterly alone in his entire life.

Miles led the bay forward through the mass of warriors. He stood twenty feet from the chief and again made the sign of peace with his outstretched hands. There was no expression on Ota Kte's red-painted face.

The wind shifted and swirled the smoke layer over the village, rifting it and driving it down the valley. The sun was

119

touching the tips of the Big Horns, and deep purple shadows were filling the valleys and draws.

Miles wet his dry lips. He could feel those murderous eyes on his back. It wasn't easy to talk with a dry throat and a pounding heart. "I have come to the village of Ota Kte to trade," he said loudly in his passable Oglala.

There was no answer. A medicine man had appeared at the door of the medicine lodge, his head fully covered by a bison bull head, horns and all. Miles had an uncanny feeling he was being watched by the actual living bull itself rather than by the medicine man.

Ota Kte folded his muscular arms over the pipebone breastplate he wore. "You speak our tongue," he said. "That is good. Then you will understand me. You have not come to the village of Ota Kte to trade, but to die, white man."

Miles wet his lips again and swallowed hard. "I have no war with Ota Kte and his Oglalas," he said.

"He lies," said a scar-faced warrior. "He is with those *Wasicun* who drive the spotted buffalo through our hunting grounds."

"That is true," said Miles. "But we did not attack you. It was you who attacked us."

Ota Kte scowled. "You talk in twisted words. Is this not *our* land? Did your people not come here unbidden? That trail was not to be used. They will die. You will die."

Miles tried not to appear excited or frightened, but it took all the control he had. "I am ready to die when it is my time to die," he said calmly. "Does Ota Kte know when he will die?"

"No man knows that," said the Oglala.

"There is a way to find out," said Miles.

It was very quiet after he spoke. Those who could hear him knew what he meant. Miles looked beyond the council lodge and the medicine lodge. A young boy stood with a rope tied about the squat, powerful body of a young badger. Miles dropped the reins of the bay and walked slowly and calmly toward the boy and his pet. Miles held out his empty hands and smiled reassuringly. He pointed to the badger and then to himself. "I want the badger," he said slowly. "Will you trade?"

The boy had no expression on his face as he stood looking up at the tall *Wasicun* who was so soon to die.

Miles took a small brass compass from his pocket and removed the small file sheathed beside his belt stone. He passed the file back and forth so that the needle followed it. The boy quickly covered his mouth in awe. Miles handed him the

120

compass and the file. The boy handed him the rope and promptly vanished amongst the many tepees.

Miles half led and half dragged the badger to the bare area before Ota Kte. The chief had been joined by some older men, likely the members of the council. The sun was fully gone now, and the only light came from the flickering fires.

Miles stood there, the firelight playing on his bronzed, seemingly fearless face. "I came here in peace, Ota Kte, and unarmed. I will need a knife. Do not be afraid." He smiled.

There was a look of scorn upon the chief's face. He walked forward, took his knife from its sheath, and handed it, handle first, to Miles. Miles could have killed him in an instant, but there was no fear upon the face of the Oglala.

Miles tested the edge of the knife as Ota Kte turned his broad back, hesitated a moment, then walked slowly to his place.

The crowd moved in closer. Miles could feel the massed heat of their bodies and smell the odor of their sweat and paint. His breath came erratically in his dry throat. He wanted to scream, to yell, to run from that place of sudden death. He raised his head. "No man knows his future," he said slowly and clearly. "There is but one way to learn how long he will live. Will Ota Kte take that way?"

There was a long silence. Ota Kte raised a hand. He looked at the badger and then at Miles. "I have no wish to know my future now," he said. "My medicine is not prepared for such a test."

It was as good a way as any of getting out of a situation, thought Miles. Miles drew the badger close, twisted the rope about his left hand, and thrust hard and true for the heart. The badger jerked and then stiffened. His claws scraped the ground, and then he was still. Miles looked up at the chief. The firelight flickered on the painted face and reflected from the pipebone breastplate. For a long moment the two men looked at each other. Then Miles knelt down, ripped the belly of the badger from one end to the other, and forced the gaping wound wide apart with his bloody hands, so that the belly formed a container for the gushing blood.

Miles stood up and calmly lighted a cigar with his bloodsmeared hands. He blew a puff of smoke to the four points of the compass, to the earth and to the sky. He folded his arms and waited. It was pure unadulterated hell to stand there waiting for the badger's blood to congeal, but there was nothing he *could* do but wait.

It was fully dark now. The odor of cooking food drifted across the village. Not a warrior moved from his position as they watched this mad *Wasicun* who had ridden so boldly into their village to face Ota Kte.

The cigar was almost gone when Miles at last removed it from his lips. Perhaps the badger's blood was not congealed enough as yet, but he couldn't wait any longer. His legs felt weak, his body was soaked with sweat. Cool as the evening was, he could feel the sweat soaking through his buckskin jacket. Miles looked up at the sky as though praying, which he certainly was, although not to the spirits of the Lakotas. He knelt beside the stiffening badger. He held the sides of the great wound with his bloody hands and looked into the cavity. Gasps of awe came from all sides, hands covered open mouths, and eyes turned quickly away. The *Wasicun* had dared all! The *Wasicun* was still alive!

Miles looked into the dark blood. He wasn't sure if he saw it then, and he would never be sure for the rest of his life, but it seemed to him that he saw a face in the jelling blood. It was the face of Miles Flint, all right, but the face of a Miles Flint who had seen many, many winters.

Miles stood up and wiped his hands on his trousers. Only the bravest of the brave amongst the Lakotas would have done such a thing. If a young face was seen reflected in the blood, they would soon die; if the face was older, they would experience many more years of life.

Ota Kte studied Miles. "You are a brave man. I will not ask you what you saw, for that is your medicine. What is it you want from the Oglalas?"

"There is a woman here," said Miles. "A squaw captured from the white men who drive the spotted buffalo north to the land of the Great White Giant. I wish to trade for her."

"You have horses? Guns? Blankets? What will you trade?"

Miles waited a moment. "I have big medicine for the Oglalas," he said. "For this big medicine, I want two things."

"You talk much," said Ota Kte. "How can a *Wasicun* have medicine for the Oglalas? Speak, and speak well, white man, for your every word will be weighed. If your words are not well, the squaws will have you this night. We will then see how brave you really are."

"I looked into the belly of the badger," said Miles. "Even if Ota Kte condemns me to death, he will let me die like a man, not like a screaming animal. This much he owes me."

A faint flicker of admiration crossed the red-painted face. "You white men are full of promises for which you give nothing," said the chief.

Miles turned, and his heart damned near stopped as he saw the massed faces behind him. It was like looking through a smoky portal into hell itself. The warriors had crowded in around the bay, and the sweetish, greasy smell of them almost sickened Miles. He rested a hand on the rolled-up buffalo pelt and motioned the nearest warriors back. He untied the bundle and carried it to the bare firelit space in front of Ota Kte, the medicine man, and the older members of the council.

The buffalo bull mask turned toward Ota Kte, the firelight glistening on the horns, and the medicine man spoke swiftly. They were too far away for Miles to catch the words, which were muffled by the mask. The medicine man stepped back, and Ota Kte looked at Miles. "This medicine you have," he said quietly. "How did you get it?"

Miles took a long chance. "*Wakan Tanka*," he said loudly.

"The white man does not have *Wakan Tanka*," said a pockmarked elder. "No white man has *Wakan Tanka!*"

Miles wet his dry lips. The ice was thin, so very thin. *Wakan Tanka* was an exalted and sacred power, an all-pervading vital force. It had no existence of its own but was a kind of quality in something already existing.

"Speak, white man," said Ota Kte.

Miles raised his hand and pointed to the east. "The sun is first amongst deities for the Lakotas, and beside it the sky, the earth, and the solid rock. Then there are the spirits of the moon, the winds, and the bison. The thunderbirds, whose beating wings make the air tremble, are gods of war and gave the Lakotas the spear and the tomahawk. These all have *Wakan Tanka*." Miles spoke loudly and earnestly, filling in his sometimes inadequate knowledge of the tongue with the gestures of the sign language, so that all might understand.

"Tell us of the *Wakan Tanka* of the *Wasicun*," said a hawk-faced warrior who stood with the elders.

"Does not the *Wasicun* have the horse and the rifle? Is this not *Wakan Tanka*? Did not the Lakotas get the horse and the rifle from the *Wasicun?*" said Miles, almost in scorn. "Any Lakota should know that!"

It was a telling blow, for Miles had spoken the truth.

Once again the bison head moved, and the medicine man spoke to Ota Kte. As the bison head turned to look at Miles he again had the uncanny feeling that an actual, living buffalo bull was looking at him.

Ota Kte eyed Miles. "You have spoken well," he said. "But you have not shown us any big medicine. Speak now. Tell us of this medicine." He pointed to the dark eastern sky. "If the moon arises before you finish, you will not leave this camp alive. Perhaps the dawn will look upon your face, if

123

you are still alive. You are strong and brave. You will live a long time under the knives of the squaws."

Miles's throat went dry. He had no idea of how much time had passed, but the moon would rise early. Perhaps even now it was almost touching the eastern sky beyond the valley of the Powder River. He could feel the tension amongst the silent Lakotas. Whatever he said or did from now on would have to impress them, or he would die, and Lorena Carlisle would face her fate alone in one of the many lodges of the village.

Miles drew in a deep breath. He raised his hands to the dark sky. "Long winters ago, during a time of great hunger, two hunters of the Sans Arc had gone out to hunt for game, which was very scarce," he said. "They were returning empty-handed when they encountered a beautiful maiden, garbed in flowing white buckskin, carrying a bundle of the holy sage." He paused. He knew the story as well as they did, but he wasn't sure whether or not he was impressing them with his knowledge. "One of the hunters had evil ideas about this beautiful maiden, but the other was of pure mind. A cloud had enveloped both of them, and when it cleared the pure-minded hunter saw his companion at his feet, a bare skeleton from which bloated, flesh-eating snakes sluggishly crawled. 'Behold!' the maiden said. 'I am coming to your people, and will bring them something of importance. Tell them to prepare for my coming.'"

The fires had died down and shadows filled in between the tepees while the smoke drifted in the now windless air, rifting about the tops of the many tepees. It was very quiet. Not a dog barked. Not a moccasin husked on the hard bare ground.

"The maiden came to the village of the Sans Arcs," continued Miles, "and to Standing Hollow Horn, who was then chief of the tribe. She gave solemn instructions, and from the bundle of holy sage she took a pipe. 'With this sacred pipe,' she said, 'you will walk the earth, which is your Mother, as the Great Mystery is your Father. The bowl of the pipe is red stone. It is the earth. Every step you take upon the earth should be as a prayer. The stem of the pipe is wood and represents all that grows upon the earth. These twelve eagle feathers that hang upon the stem are from the Spotted Eagle and represent all the winged things of the air. All the things of the universe are joined to you who smoke this pipe. All send their voices to the Great Mystery, for when you pray with this pipe you pray *for* and *with* everything!'"

Miles did not dare turn to look at the eastern sky, but it seemed to him as though the sky overhead and to the west was a little lighter, as though receiving some of the light of the rising moon.

"She gave the pipe to Standing Hollow Horn and said, 'Behold this pipe! Always remember that it is sacred and treat it as such, for it will take you to the end of time. I am leaving you now, but I shall always watch over your people. At the end I shall return to you again,'" spoke Miles in a slow, earnest tone. He was sure now the moon was touching the eastern sky beyond the valley of the Powder.

Miles still had the knife given to him by Ota Kte. He did not look at the impassive faces ringing him on each side. "The maiden then walked away to a hill, where she sat down. She arose as a white buffalo and trotted over the hill out of sight of the Sans Arcs." Miles bent swiftly, before he could be stopped, and slashed through the thrums that bound together the snow-back buffalo pelt. He gripped the cured hide and flipped it, unrolling it on the bare earth, so that it fell outer side upward almost at the moccasined feet of Ota Kte. The firelight shone on the albino hair.

There were awestruck gasps from the massed Lakotas. Hands covered opened mouths. The sacred Buffalo Calf Pipe was still in possession of the same band of Sans Arcs to whom the maiden had appeared, handed down from generation to generation always within the same blood. *It was the most sacred object of the Sioux Nation,* wrapped always in the purifying sage and treated with the utmost awe and respect.

The die was cast. If Ota Kte accepted the albino hide, no harm would come to Miles, for did he not possess *Wakan Tanka* to have found such a sacred object? To harm him might spoil the medicine of the hide.

Ota Kte looked at Miles and then at his people. Three bucks came from the crowd, and the oldest of them spoke to the chief. Miles knew them. They were the three who had moved in on him unseen the day he had killed the snow-back. They knew he had killed the snow-back.

Ota Kte held up a hand. "You are free, *Wasicun,*" he said. "You may leave in peace from the village of Ota Kte."

"And the woman?" said Miles.

Ota Kte spoke to a brave, who trotted off behind the council lodge. The chief folded his arms and studied Miles. There was a faint trace of admiration on his strong face. "The way is open to the north," he said. "Drive the spotted buffalo away from our hunting grounds. No harm will come to them and to the *Wasicun* who drive them. *But do not come back, Wasicun.* If you do, your medicine will not protect you."

Miles held out the chief's hunting knife, but Ota Kte shook

125

his head. "It is yours," he said. His meaning was plain enough. As one brave man to another, the knife was the parting gift of Ota Kte.

Miles turned on his heel just as the moon revealed itself, softly filling the eastern sky. He led the bay through the Lakotas, who parted respectfully to let him make his way.

He saw her beyond the crowd, standing by herself, dressed in the softest of white buckskin, beaded moccasins on her tiny feet, her hair braided in the style of the women of the Lakotas. He led the bay to her, picked her up and easily lifted her to the cantle of the bay. He mounted, feeling her arms creep about his waist. "Miles, Miles," she said softly. She pressed her tear-stained face against his broad back.

He guided the bay through the empty streets of the village. He rode through the dark timber into the grassy valley, now filling with the light of the rising moon. Miles rode toward the distant valley of the Crazy Woman. He did not look back. There was nothing to fear now.

CHAPTER FOURTEEN

The first snowfall of the year drifted through the gray skies over the great valley of the Gallatin as almost three thousand head of longhorns who had been driven almost three thousand miles from Texas, starting in April—the Moon of the Red Grass Appearing, in the language of the Lakotas—and now it was November—the Moon of Falling Leaves—and almost the time of December—the Moon of Popping Trees—walked the last mile of their journey.

Since leaving the crossing of the Crazy Woman, the longhorns, still led by Old Brimstone and his clear-sounding bell, had moved north, always north, leaving the Powder River for the Tongue River, turning westerly toward the Little Big Horn and then the Big Horn itself, then northwest to the fording of the Yellowstone. They passed through Emigrant Gap to reach Bozeman and the valley of the Gallatin.

Chip Macklin had been sent many days ahead to the Carlisle land grant to hire men to build the ranch buildings, according to the plan Jonas Carlisle had carried with him from Texas.

They would be ready by the time the heavy snows fell. Ghost Face would be early that year, but Lorena Carlisle and the Carlisle corrida as well as the thousands of longhorns would be ready for it.

The ringing of axes and the whining of saws drifted through the swirling snow as the last of the longhorns came to a half in a sheltered area where grass could still be found. The clapper of Old Brimstone's bell was tied down permanently after the thousands of miles it had rung to guide the trail herd to its new home in Montana territory.

The chuckwagon, the Studebakers, and the supply wagons, creaking and groaning, rolling on thin iron tires, were driven to the ranchsite, close to the new buildings, and the teams were unhitched. The remuda was driven to the fenced pasture and turned loose.

Miles Flint rode through the swirling snow to where Lorena Carlisle stood beside Beck Sterret, looking at the rapidly rising buildings. Miles swung down from the bay and took off his hat. "I'll be riding on to Virginia City," he said.

Lorena Carlisle nodded. She had been expecting this.

Beck Sterret looked up the great valley. "I doubt if Texas could beat this for cattle country," he said, almost as though to himself.

"Beck and all the drivers are staying on," said Lorena.

Miles raised his eyebrows. "I thought the Texans could hardly wait to return to the Lone Star State," he said in mock surprise.

Beck shrugged. "We intend to become Montanans," he said. "Somebody has to people this coming state. Yuh can hardly get better blood to do it then Texans, can yuh?"

"*Ex*-Texans," said Miles. "I'll have to agree with that."

"Yuh won't stay on then?" said the trail boss.

"No," said Miles. "I'm not a cattleman."

"The buffalo won't last forever," said Lorena. She looked at Miles. "Beck is staying with me to foreman the ranch."

"You won't find a better man," said Miles.

"*Gracias*," said the Texan.

"*Por nada*," said Miles.

Miles took her hand in his. "Good-bye," he said.

She looked at him for a long moment. "Good-bye, Miles." She turned and walked to the front of her Studebaker.

Miles thrust out a hand to Beck. "Good-bye," he said.

The hard hand of the Texan gripped that of Miles. "Good-bye, Miles," he said quietly.

Miles swung up on the bay. It was the first time in the long months since he had known Beck Sterret that the trail boss had called him by his first name. He touched the bay with his heels and rode toward the road that led to the Madison and then to Virginia City.

Beck's spurs chimed softly as he walked to Lorena. "He'll be back, Mis' Carlisle," he said. "He'll be back when the grass first shows itself in the spring."

She did not answer or indicate that she agreed. She knew why Miles Flint had not stayed on in the valley of the Gallatin. Jonas Carlisle was not long dead. Miles had given her time, but he would be back in May, in the Moon When the Ponies Shed. Her medicine told her that.